STORM CHASER

STORM CHASER

CHRIS PLATT

PEACHTREE
ATLANTA

Ω
Published by
PEACHTREE PUBLISHERS
1700 Chattahoochee Avenue
Atlanta, Georgia 30318-2112

www.peachtree-online.com

Cover design by Loraine M. Joyner
Book design by Melanie McMahon Ives

Printed in the United States of America
10 9 8 7 6 5 4 3 2 1
First Edition

Paint horse photo on page 175 by Jessica Hein, courtesy of American Paint Horse Association (APHA)

Library of Congress Cataloging-in-Publication Data

Platt, Chris, 1959-
Storm Chaser / written by Chris Platt.
p. cm.
Summary: When a fire forces her family to turn their home into a guest ranch, aspiring horse trainer Jessica finds herself working once again with her favorite horse, Storm Chaser, to tame the wild filly for snobbish, spoiled Ariel, Storm Chaser's future owner.
ISBN 978-1-56145-496-9 / 1-56145-496-6
[1. Horses–Training–Fiction. 2. Ranch life–Fiction.] I. Title.
PZ7.P7123115St 2009
[Fic]–dc22

2008052840

To Brandon, in hopes that you'll soon be working on that great book idea. You've got the talent. Just do it!

ONE

"Jessie, get down!" Thirteen-year-old Jessica Warner ducked behind the gate and tried to make herself as small as possible as her father drove the herd of horses toward the pen. She knew better than to stand out there like a warning flag flopping in the wind. If the new horses saw her, they would swerve off the path and refuse to enter the capture pen.

The pounding of hooves grew to a thunderous roar as the herd approached the gate. Jessica could feel the vibration under her feet. She pushed her long, dark hair from her eyes and peered through the boards. Screams of "Yah, yah!" echoed from the men driving the horses forward.

It was her job to slam the gate closed once the horses were inside. Her heart galloped in her chest and she took a deep breath, praying she'd get the door closed before any of the horses circled the pen and tried to run back out.

Jessica could see her older brother Duncan and his two friends from the nearby reservation, Gator and Wyatt Lightfoot, riding their horses into positions at the sides of the herd.

They waved their hats to keep the young quarter horses moving toward the pen.

From where she crouched, Jessica saw mostly bays—with their shiny brown coats and black manes and tails—and bright red chestnuts. There were also a couple of grays, a blue roan, and the most beautiful black-and-white paint she'd ever seen.

The horses were three and four years old, and had been running on high mountain pasture on the Northern Nevada Reservation for the last several years. They'd been weaned and handled at six months of age, but left wild ever since.

Wild Hawk Ranch, which belonged to Jessica's family, bought fifteen horses each summer from the Paiute Reservation, and broke them to sell to local ranchers and rodeo competitors. Duncan and the Lightfoot boys did most of the work, and Jessica watched them every chance she got. Someday she hoped to be as good as they were at training horses.

Jessica knew she could do it, if only they'd give her a chance. She loved her father and brother, but for the last couple of years, whenever she'd asked to help with the training, they'd waved her off, saying she was still too young. But Duncan had been helping their father since he was eleven. It wasn't fair. She considered herself plenty old enough to train horses. Maybe her family and the Lightfoot boys didn't know it yet, but *this* was going to be her year.

Every muscle in Jessica's body tensed as the herd bore down upon the holding corral. She could see the wide-flared nostrils of the lead horses, their sides heaving, tired from their headlong run across the mountain. She put her hands on the gate and kept a low profile, hardly daring to breathe as the first quarter horse entered the pen.

The surprised cries of several horses rang out when they realized they were trapped. The blue roan in the lead circled around, looking for a way out. The dust they churned beneath their powerful hooves rose so thickly Jessica had to squint to see. When the last horse crossed the threshold she pushed the gate with all her might, slamming it closed just as the roan galloped near.

"Good job, Jess!" Duncan yelled above the clamor of frightened whinnies and pounding hooves.

Gator, the seventeen-year-old Lightfoot boy, gave Jessica a thumbs-up. Wyatt, the younger brother, smiled shyly at her as he led his golden palomino gelding over to the water trough.

Jessica felt her cheeks warm. The handsome Paiute boy with the shiny black hair and laughing eyes was fifteen, her brother's age. She'd grown up with Gator and Wyatt and thought of them as family. But lately, whenever Wyatt smiled at her, she got a funny feeling in the pit of her stomach. She looked away quickly, turning her attention to the horses—especially the black-and-white filly.

Mr. Warner stepped down off his horse and patted Jessica on the back. "You did good, girl. I couldn't have done a better job myself."

Jessica beamed at the words of praise. "I can do more," she said, crossing her fingers for luck. "I'm old enough to help out with the breaking now, Dad. I've watched you guys train horses for years. I want to learn and help out this year."

Mr. Warner rubbed the stubble on his chin and gave his

daughter an appraising look. "Jess, I'm just not sure if you're ready yet, honey. It's a dangerous job working with these wild youngsters. You could get hurt."

Jessica's heart fell to the desert sand at her feet. She sucked in a big gulp of warm air, feeling the backs of her eyes sting. *Great.* All she needed was to cry in front of her dad and the boys. That would just prove her father's point.

"But Duncan started helping four years ago." she said, taking another deep breath, willing herself not to cry.

From the corner of her eye, she could see the boys looking at the ground and scuffing their boots, clearly feeling uncomfortable witnessing her dilemma. She crossed her arms and looked up at her father, staring him straight in the eye. "I can do it. I know I can."

Her father reached out and put his big hand on her head. Jessica frowned. Having her father treat her like a little kid in front of the boys was almost worse than having him say no.

"Give me a few days to think about this, Jess, okay?" her father said. "For now, go on up to the house and see if your mother needs any help. I've got to get these horses settled in and fed."

Jessica turned and walked to the house, her back ramrod stiff.

"See ya, Jessie," Wyatt called after her, but Jessica didn't trust herself to speak. She waved her hand in the air and continued toward the house.

She found her mother in the laundry room, folding towels. "Do you need some help, Mom?"

Mrs. Warner shook her head and smiled. "No, thanks. I

can get these." She nodded toward the living room. "I know you're dying to call Marybeth and tell her about the new horses, so go ahead."

Jessica hesitated in the doorway. "Mom, do you think I could help Dad and the boys train the horses this year?"

Her mother stared at her a moment, sizing her up. Then she nodded. "I think so, Jess, but you know the decision is up to your father. Horse breaking is his department."

"Thanks, Mom." Jessica ran out of the room, but her mother called her back. Jessica poked her head around the door and got pelted with a fluffy washcloth.

"Better wash your face before Wyatt sees you looking like a crow in a mud bath," Mrs. Warner teased.

"Mom!" Jessica protested. "I don't care what Wyatt thinks about *anything!*" As soon as the words came out of her mouth, she knew they were untrue. Okay, maybe she did care…but not that much.

She quickly washed her face and then picked up the phone to call her friend Marybeth, who lived a half-mile down the road at Thunder Mountain Ranch. Marybeth was three years younger and could be a little annoying sometimes, but she was the only girl close to Jessica's age who lived nearby.

Jessica had a few friends who lived in the smaller towns on the other side of the valley, but she only saw them at school. She didn't hear much from them in the summer. Marybeth got under her skin sometimes, but one thing was for sure: they both loved horses!

Jessica dialed her number but kept getting a busy signal.

That usually meant Marybeth or one of her brothers was hogging the computer. Their family had an old dial-up account just like the Warners did. She hung up the phone and turned on own her computer to send Marybeth an e-mail.

The open window allowed a breeze to drift through the warm house. It was the beginning of June. School had been out for a few days, and the heat was already beginning.

She began typing her message, breathing in the sweet scent of high desert sagebrush. Then a sudden rumbling noise caught her attention. She paused with her hands over the keyboard, listening to the sound of a vehicle making its way down Wild Hawk Ranch's long gravel driveway.

Jessica brushed her hair over her shoulder and leaned forward to peek out of the family room window. She frowned at the fancy SUV with the large decal on the door bumping up the road. Her father would not be pleased.

She dropped the curtain back into place and returned to the computer, squinting her green eyes as she quickly finished her e-mail. A car door slammed in the driveway just as Jessica hit Send. She had more to tell Marybeth, but at the moment, the prospect of watching her father do battle with yet another travel agent seemed more exciting.

She shut down the computer and ran out the side door to the large poplar tree that grew in the middle of the lawn.

Shep, their black-and-white Border collie, rushed from the barn, barking at the stranger. A moment later Mr. Warner walked through the stable door. He stretched his tall lanky body and ran a calloused hand through his short sandy hair, scowling as he walked forward to greet the unwelcome visitor.

Jessica dropped to her knees, busying herself with pulling cheat grass from the patch of pink flowers that circled the tree. She didn't want to just stand around and stare. Her mother would scold her for being rude if she got caught. The May rains had made the weeds grow just as plentifully as the flowers, and pulling weeds gave her a good reason to be close enough to eavesdrop.

She plucked a dandelion and watched the familiar scene unfold. A lady in a well-tailored business suit got out of the car and walked forward with her hand extended. Being a gentleman, her father shook it, but that's where the courtesy ended. As usual, the travel agent offered her father a deal on using Wild Hawk Ranch as a guest ranch for city-folk vacationers—or dudes, as they liked to call them out here in the country. And, as usual, her father offered the travel agent an immediate escort back to her vehicle.

Jessica rocked on her heels, tossing a clump of cheat grass over her shoulder as she watched the well-dressed woman drive off. She wouldn't mind having guests around the ranch. It was so lonely here with only her brother and Marybeth to keep her company.

Duncan—whom she fondly called "Dunce" on occasion—with his quiet personality, didn't make a good companion. Trying to get him to talk was like waiting for lightning to strike the same spot twice—it rarely happened. Marybeth dropped by for visits every week, but her company got old fast. Sometimes it seemed like she'd never go home.

Jessica stood and brushed the dirt from her knees as she watched the vehicle disappear down the road. Her father turned to her with hands on hips and gave her a knowing stare.

"You heard?" Her father slapped his cowboy hat on the leg of his faded jeans and cued the Border collie to sit.

Jessica bobbed her head and kicked at the dirt beneath her tennis shoes. She knew what her father would say next. The words were always the same.

"This is our home." Mr. Warner waved an arm toward the old two-story brick house, the large wooden barn, and the scattering of bunkhouses and out buildings. "I'm not going to have a bunch of strangers roaming over my property, getting into things that don't belong to them." He paused, smoothing the mustache that ran across his upper lip and down to his chin. "Especially if they're city folk. I don't cotton much to people who don't know about animals or working the land."

Jessica nodded and returned to the house to help her mother with the evening meal. She knew her father would never give in, but it was still nice to dream about having guests. It would be fun having somebody else to hang out with and go riding with over the fields and mountains. Sometimes Duncan went with her. But Jessica's chestnut horse, Rusty, was really old, and Duncan's young mount liked to race the wind. She might as well be riding by herself with Duncan so far ahead of her.

"Why the long face, Jess?" Mrs. Warner placed a pan of homemade bread dough in the large oven as she eyed her daughter curiously. She wiped her hands on her apron and blew a lock of reddish hair off her forehead. "Come on, out with it," she said with a smile.

Jessica pulled a chair up to the large counter that stood in the middle of the kitchen and began snapping the pile of string beans that lay on the cutting board. "We just had another visit from a travel agent."

Mrs. Warner took the chair next to her daughter and reached for a handful of beans. "And what did your father say? Let me guess."

Jessica grinned. "Well, he was more polite to this one, probably because she was a woman, but he said the same thing he always does." Jessica deepened her voice and did a perfect imitation of her father.

Mrs. Warner laughed. "You really shouldn't poke fun at your dad like that, honey. You know he wants what's best for us."

Jessica snapped a bean into three sections, tossing them into the strainer. "What do you think, Mom? What if we turned Wild Hawk into a guest ranch?"

Mrs. Warner looked down at the counter, busying her hands with the beans. "I think it might be a good thing if we did it on a limited basis. I've had an agent or two catch me when your father wasn't home. They talk a good game, and they gave me a lot of information on what it would take to turn Wild Hawk Ranch into a vacation place."

Jessica kept quiet as her mother stared out the big kitchen window to where her dad and Duncan were unloading hay at the end of the barn.

"Lord knows it has been a tough year," her mother sighed. "Beef prices are down. Feed costs are up. And I hear the Bureau of Land Management is talking about raising the grazing fees again. If we don't get this year's calves fattened up enough to get a good price out of them, we're going to be in trouble. We could use a little extra help."

"We've got those empty cabins out back," Jessica said. "It wouldn't hurt to clean a couple of them out and use them. I think it would be fun to have some new people around here."

Mrs. Warner dried her hands on her apron, then ran a loving hand over her daughter's hair. "I know it gets lonely out here for you, Jess. Marybeth's a little too young, and Duncan's got Wyatt and Gator." She picked up the bowl of snapped beans and took them to the pot of boiling water on the stove. "It's a good thing you've got your horse."

Jessica smiled. Her parents had given her Rusty on her third birthday. He'd been old even back then. Now that she was thirteen, poor old Rusty needed to retire. His gaits were slow and most of his energy gone, but she still loved him with all her heart.

"Go tell your father and brother that supper will be ready in about forty-five minutes," Mrs. Warner said. "That should give them enough time to finish stacking the hay in the barn." She winked at Jessie. "And if you hurry, you could probably get old Rusty brushed and have plenty of time left to make friends with that pretty little paint filly I saw you eyeing."

Jessica grabbed a couple of carrots from the refrigerator and headed for the horses. Duncan was just pulling the tractor and empty flatbed trailer from the end of the barn. They'd gotten an early crop of hay this year. They might be able to get an extra cutting by the end of the season. That would mean extra money in the bank. Jessica didn't know a lot about finances, but she knew her parents struggled to keep the ranch afloat.

Mr. Warner climbed down from the loft, dusting his hands on his shirt front. "That does it. All the hay from the first crop is in the barn," he said with a satisfied smile. "We were lucky to have such an early spring." He shaded his eyes and looked toward the nearby mountains and the gathering clouds. "And not a moment too soon. Looks like we might be in for a summer storm."

Duncan parked the trailer, then walked to the nearest horse trough and dunked his head into the cool water, shaking his blond hair like a wet dog when he stood up.

Jessica squealed, holding up her hands. "Thanks a lot, Dunce" She saw the grin cross her brother's lips and bounced a piece of carrot off his noggin. Duncan just laughed as he caught the carrot chunk and popped it into his mouth, crunching the tidbit like one of his horses.

Jessica smiled to herself as her brother turned and gazed at the gathering clouds. Duncan liked nothing better than to ride his horse into a storm. She saw the longing on his face, but her father shook his head and pushed Duncan toward the house. She hoped that someday her brother would invite her to go on a storm ride with him. The thought both scared and excited her.

A nicker drew Jessica's attention and she turned to the pen that held the new horses. The young stock in the corral snorted and huddled at the far end of the pen, but the paint filly stepped near the fence and pricked her ears, staring curiously.

Jessica grinned. Wyatt would call that a sign. She felt it, too. A plan began to form in her mind, and she put a little extra spring in her step as she walked to Rusty's stall.

She stopped in front of the stall and scratched Rusty on the neck as he leaned his head over the door to accept the carrot. She'd been honing her riding talents on the old gelding for years, dreaming of the day she could join her father and brother in the training pen. Somehow, some way, she was going to convince her father to let her train this year.

Her first project would be the beautiful paint filly.

TWO

"Mom said dinner would be ready soon," Jessica called to her father as she gathered the bucket of brushes outside Rusty's stall.

Mr. Warner climbed down from the loft and dusted off his jeans. "Don't be long," he cautioned. "The wind is picking up out there." He waved to Jessica and followed Duncan up the path to the old brick house on the rise.

Jessica let herself into Rusty's stall. "Hey, old man, how are you doing?" She hugged his neck and scratched the chestnut gelding behind the ears, laughing when he nudged her pockets looking for the treat he knew she would bring.

She broke the carrot into several pieces, feeding them to him one at a time. Rusty munched them slowly and purposefully. At twenty-two years of age, his teeth weren't as good as they used to be.

Jessica pulled out the rubber curry comb and rubbed it in circles across Rusty's swayed back. The gelding cocked his hind leg and sighed. Jessica lost herself in thought while she swirled the curry over the horse's body. She knew her aging friend wouldn't be rideable for much longer. She had overheard her mother and father talking about getting her another horse when they could afford it. She smiled. Maybe it would be that pretty black-and-white filly.

She closed her eyes, imagining the feel of wind in her hair as she galloped through the valleys on the swift little paint. She'd be able to keep up with Duncan if she were to get the new filly, no problem.

Rusty blew through his lips, bringing Jessica back from her daydreams. She looked into the old gelding's soft brown eyes, feeling guilty for even thinking of replacing him. She threw her arms around his neck again, breathing in the warm horse scent, then kissed him on his whiskered muzzle. "We'll keep riding as long as you feel up to it," she promised.

Jessica glanced at her watch. She had just enough time for a quick visit to the corral before she had to wash up for dinner. She put away the brush box and grabbed the last carrot, then headed out the barn door to the large pen that stood on the east side of the barn.

The young horses tossed their heads and snorted when Jessica approached. They trotted nervously to the other end of the pen and stood with their heads high, their nostrils distended to catch her scent.

Jessica looked over the fifteen beautifully muscled animals that stood in the corral, pawing the ground and eyeing her suspiciously as they milled about the enclosure.

Wyatt and Gator, under the guidance of their father, were the horse breeders for the reservation. They knew the animals well and chose their stallions and mares with care. The resulting offspring were perfect examples of American quarter horses and paints. The young horses had broad and well-muscled chests, short strong backs, and powerful hindquarters. Their small, perfectly formed heads had pronounced jaws and kind, intelligent eyes.

Most of the ranchers in the area owned Lightfoot horses that her father and brother had trained. They proved invaluable for ranch work. Their ability to carry a rider all day and twist and turn sharply to work cattle made them a favorite of local cattle ranchers.

"Easy, there," Jessica said. The skittish animals' ears flicked back and forth at the sound of her voice. Several of the horses pushed deeper into the herd, but the little paint filly took one step forward, her petite muzzle extending to catch a better scent of the carrot Jessica offered.

She held the carrot out for several minutes, but the filly refused to come any closer. Jessica sighed and tossed the carrot into the pen. The little filly jumped when it hit the ground near her hooves. Jessica backed up a few steps and watched the paint lower her nose to the ground, poking at the carrot before biting off a piece.

The filly bobbed her pretty head and spit parts of the carrot back onto the ground. Jessica covered her mouth to keep her giggle from spooking the filly. "Don't worry," she whispered as she turned toward the house. "Someday you'll learn to love carrots."

She ran across the backyard, covering the distance to the house in no time. At least she had made a connection with the beautiful paint—if only to offer the horse a treat she didn't like. It was a start.

The family was just sitting down to dinner when Jessica entered the back door. Already her parents seemed to be in a heated debate. She stopped short. It was unusual to hear her parents argue.

"Hurry up, Jess," her father said, noticing her in the doorway. "You're late."

Jessica hurriedly washed her hands and slipped into her spot opposite her brother. Duncan's blue eyes bounced back and forth between their parents as they discussed turning the Wild Hawk into a guest ranch.

"I won't have it," their father said as he heaped a large portion of mashed potatoes onto his plate. "As long as we can make a living running cattle and selling some of our hay crop, I won't have strangers staying on my land—cold cash or not."

The lights flickered and everyone glanced at the ceiling to see if they would stay on. The wind had picked up heavily and there was no longer a doubt that a major storm was on its way.

"All right, enough of this conversation," Mrs. Warner said, handing a plate of chicken-fried steak to Jessica. A loud clap of thunder shook the walls of the house. "Let's worry about getting dinner eaten before the lights go out. Are all the horses in?" Mrs. Warner asked.

Duncan nodded, stuffing a big bite of broccoli into his mouth.

"All except the new horses," Mr. Warner said. "But they've

got that big tree that hangs over part of their pen. They can gather under that just like they'd do if they were living wild back on reservation land."

"The cattle are in the outer fields," Mrs. Warner said. "Will they be okay there if the storm hits?"

Mr. Warner nodded. "They'll be safe enough. I'm glad they're not out on the range, or they could spook and scatter all over the mountain. The last time that happened, it took us a month of searching to gather them all up, and we lost a few of them. We can't afford to lose a single head this year."

The meal ended with the din of shutters banging in the high wind and more flickering from the lights. A few drops of rain hit the window, but for the most part, this was a dry storm full of wind, thunder, and lightning.

When the lights finally went out for good at about nine o'clock, Jessica decided she might as well go to bed early. Her parents weren't doing a lot of talking after their argument over the guest ranch, and Duncan never was much of a conversationalist.

"I'm going to check the horses before bed," she called as she lifted her jacket from the peg in the hallway and pulled on her boots.

"Be careful," her mother cautioned. "Would you like your brother to go with you?"

Jessica shook her head. "I'll take Shep." She signaled the Border collie to follow and stepped into the dark, stormy night. Standing on the back porch, she lifted her nose to sniff the air. The wind whipped through her hair, blowing it

trying to get her bearings. Shep whimpered outside her door, then scratched again. She sat up, sniffing at the strange acrid smell in the air. An odd flickering of light cast an eerie glow outside of her bedroom window.

Jessica slipped from her bed, noting the silence of the night. The storm had passed. She tiptoed across the room and peeked through the curtains, then gasped as her heart tumbled in her chest. The odd glow of light illuminating the night was the orange flicker of flames rising from the old wooden barn. Wild Hawk Ranch was on fire!

THREE

Jessica stumbled in the darkness of her room, her heart climbing into her throat. "Mom!" she cried. "Dad! Duncan!" She fumbled for the light switch. Her fingers found the switch and light flooded the room. At least the electricity was back on.

"What is it, Jess?" Duncan pushed open her door, his eyes sliding to the window where the eerie light flickered in the reflection of the glass.

"Duncan, get Mom and Dad. The barn's on fire!" Jessica grabbed her jeans and shirt as her brother's footsteps pounded down the stairway. Her hands shook so badly she had trouble dressing herself. She shoved one leg into her jeans and shifted off-balance, almost falling to the floor. Dragging the shirt over her head, she ran down the stairs after Duncan.

Shep barked furiously. Her mother and father were just leaving their bedroom when she reached the bottom of the staircase. "The horses are in the barn!" Jessica cried.

"Call 911, Jess!" Mr. Warner shouted as he ran across the room. He grabbed his hat off the wall peg and slammed it down tight on his head, shouldering the back door open. "It may be too late for the barn, but we might need the fire department for the house."

The house? Jessica felt her stomach turn inside-out and her legs go weak. Her dad was right. They were a long way from town. The barn would probably be gone by the time the fire trucks arrived.

Duncan grabbed her shoulder to steady her. "Don't worry, sis, the barn is a ways from here. The house should be okay. I'll help get the horses out. The cattle will be all right where they are." He turned and ran out the back door.

Jessica's throat squeezed closed. Duncan had just spoken more words in one standing than he'd said all day. That alone told her they were in deep trouble. It would be bad enough losing the barn and next winter's feed supply, but what would they do if they lost the horses and their house, too? What if she lost Rusty?

She walked across the floor to the phone, feeling as if she were moving in slow motion. Her feet seemed to be filled with lead. She lifted the receiver and punched in the emergency number. Her hands trembled so much, she wasn't sure she'd hit the right buttons, but a moment later, the calm voice of the emergency operator spoke up. Jessica gave the woman the information she requested, then hung up the phone and ran to join her family outside.

When she came face-to-face with the awful reality of the raging barn fire, she froze in her tracks, choking as the wind shifted, blowing the billowing dark clouds of acrid smoke toward them. She rubbed her eyes, trying to peer into the bright flames. How much of the building was on fire?

Sparks and ash rained down on Jessica while her eyes traced the line of flames. The fire seemed to have started at the back of the stable. A cold sweat dampened her forehead when she realized that the horses were in that part of the barn. And Rusty was one of them!

Fear roared in her ears, drowning out the awful sound of the crackling pops as the old wooden structure continued to succumb to the voracious fire. "Rusty's in there!" she screamed, racing forward to open the barn doors.

Jessica felt strong hands around her waist and her feet lifted off the ground. Her father carried her back and set her none too gently next to her mother. "Stay here," he commanded. The sound of frightened whinnies floated on the night air as she stared into her father's worried face.

"You can't go in there, Jess!" Mr. Warner yelled over the roar of the spreading flames. "It's too dangerous!"

"B-but…the horses…" Jessica stammered.

Her mother hugged her tightly. "Hush now, Jess," she said.

Then a movement over her father's shoulder caught Jessica's eye. A black shadow headed toward the front of the barn. She widened her eyes in the darkness, trying to make out the shape.

The front doors of the barn flew open. Jessica knew her brother was going to try to save the horses. "Duncan!" she cried.

Mr. Warner's head snapped around when Jessica shouted her brother's name. He gave her a look meant to keep her rooted to the spot, then turned and ran toward his son. "Duncan, don't you go in there!" But it was too late. Duncan's shadowy form slipped into the burning barn.

Jessica turned to her mother, seeing fear leap into her eyes. "What do we do?"

"Grab the hose!" her mother ordered. "I'll get the one from the outbuilding. We'll water down the front of the barn so they'll have a place to come out."

Jessica could sense the terror in her mother's words even though her voice remained calm and steady. She took a deep breath, trying to calm her own fears. She had to be brave, too. Her brother's and father's lives could very well depend on it. She hurried to the faucet and turned the water on full, then stretched the hose to the front of the barn, aiming the spray at the opening.

"Somebody's coming," Mrs. Warner nodded toward the long dirt road that led to their property.

Jessica saw the wildly bouncing headlights as the vehicle came pell-mell up the bumpy road. "I think it's the Lightfoots coming to help," she said.

"Good," Mrs. Warner directed her spray of water toward the barn. "I just hope the fire department gets here soon."

Jessica could hear the frightened neighs of the horses trapped in the barn. Her heart went out to them. What if they were too scared to leave the barn? But she knew her father and brother. They would find a way to bring the horses out safely. She chewed at her bottom lip, praying her father and Duncan were okay.

Another terrified whinny pierced the night and Jessica immediately recognized it. *Rusty!*

"Don't worry, honey." Mrs. Warner laid a reassuring hand her daughter's shoulder. "Duncan and your father will get all the horses out."

Tires skidded on gravel as the old blue pickup braked to a halt and Wyatt, Gator, and their father jumped from the vehicle to help.

"Thank goodness!" Mrs. Warner cried. "Jake and Duncan are in the barn, trying to get the horses out. We're keeping the doorway watered down so they'll be able to make it out." She stared at the building that was now half in flames. "We'll have to hurry. That roof won't hold out much longer."

Gator took the hose from Mrs. Warner. "Why don't you get a couple of blankets we can wet down in case the guys need them when they come out?" He peered into the roaring inferno. "If they're not out in another minute, my dad and I will go in after them."

Mrs. Warner grabbed the young boy by the arm. "Gator, I can't let you and your father risk it. There are already two men in there. It's too dangerous to send anyone else in." She jumped as the barn creaked and several boards from the loft broke through to the bottom floor in a flurry of sparks and flames. "They'll be out soon, I know it!"

A siren wailed in the distance. Everyone turned to see flashing red lights making steady progress toward the ranch.

"The fire engines are coming!" Wyatt hollered over the roar of the fire.

Just then a shout erupted from the barn. "Stand clear!" Mr. Warner's voice rang out. "One horse coming out!"

The small crowd outside the barn scattered as Mr. Warner's big bay bolted from the barn, his eyes rolling in terror as he raced away from the burning building. A moment later, the two men emerged from the barn. Duncan led his blindfolded horse while his father pushed from behind. The panicked animal stumbled through the doorway, making it forty feet from the barn before collapsing onto his side in the grass, his breath coming in great, labored gasps.

With her family safe, Jessica's spirits soared. But her eyes quickly scanned the confusion, looking for the last horse. "Where's Rusty?" she cried.

The fire engines roared into the driveway, sending up a cloud of dust that mingled with the heavy smoke from the burning barn.

"Is everyone accounted for?" the first firefighter on the scene asked, signaling his men to unroll the large hoses.

"We're all okay," Mr. Warner answered.

Jessica took several steps toward the barn. "My horse!" she screamed. "Rusty is still in the barn!" Fear seized her, choking the breath from her body. She couldn't let Rusty die like that. She took several more steps, feeling a blast of hot air as several more boards from the loft crashed to the main floor, bringing down burning bales of hay in a shower of sparks.

"Jessie!" Duncan grabbed her from behind, picking her up and carrying her backward. "Rusty wouldn't come out, Jess. He was too scared." Duncan broke into a coughing fit, doubling over and resting his hands on his thighs. When the fit passed, he raised his soot-covered face to his sister. "I tried my best, Jess, but he wouldn't go through the barn."

Mr. Warner clapped a hand on Jessica's shoulder. She wasn't sure if it was to comfort her or to keep her from dashing into the burning building to save her horse.

"Rusty's okay, Jessica. His stall door must have blown closed during the storm," Mr. Warner said. "I opened it and he went out into the corral. He's at the back of his pen, but we've got to get him out of there before the barn falls."

"Stay here, Jess," Mrs. Warner ordered. "Let your father go after Rusty."

Her father nodded, then began to wheeze uncontrollably.

"We need a medic over here!" one of the firemen yelled, signaling to the others.

Jessica waited until someone came to look after her father, then took that moment of confusion to dash to the back of the barn where Rusty's corral stood. As she approached, she heard the nervous whinnies of the new horses in the round pen. Shielding her eyes from the bright yellow and orange flames leaping skyward, she could see the youngsters were a little further away from the barn than Rusty. They would be safe for the moment. Right now, she had to direct all of her attention toward her old horse.

"Rusty?" Jessica could just make out his dark shape against the inferno. The horse pushed against the boards of his pen, his eyes wide with terror as he tried to escape the flames.

She rushed into his pen. "Rusty, come on!" She sprinted to his side, pushing him toward the exit. Rusty balked, afraid to move from his spot. Jessica cried out in alarm as a live ash landed on her horse's back and his coat began to smolder. She used her sleeve to brush off the hot ash, then pounded on Rusty's back until the fire was out. The smell of burning hair hung heavily on the air, causing her stomach to roll.

"Rusty, please," Jessica begged as she continued to push on his hind quarters. She had to get him to leave his pen before the burning barn collapsed into his corral.

Wyatt appeared by Jessica's side with a halter in his outstretched hand. "Put this on him, Jess," he instructed.

Jessica looked up in relief, managing a small smile. Wyatt was great with horses. He'd know what to do. "He won't budge," she cried in panic, fumbling with the buckle on the halter.

Wyatt positioned himself behind the old horse. "Just get the halter on him, Jess, and get out of the way. I'll make sure he moves."

Jessica's fingers shook so badly, it took several tries to get the halter latched. "Okay, he's ready. What do you want me to do?"

"Get his head pointed toward the door, then stand back!" Wyatt hollered above the crackling of the flames.

Jessica did as she was told. She pulled on the lead rope, pointing Rusty's head toward the gate, then stepped through the opening to wait for Wyatt to work a miracle. She watched as the tall, thin boy took off his baseball hat and smacked it down on Rusty's haunches, then raised his arms in the air and hollered something in Paiute.

Rusty balked, but Wyatt smacked him harder on the rear and jumped up and down, waving his arms wildly. The old gelding rushed through the gate, stumbling close on Jessica's heels as she raced away from the barn.

When they were a safe distance away, Jessica stopped and threw her arms around Rusty's neck, burying her face into his sweating coat. She could smell the fear emanating from the old horse's body. It mixed with the scent of wood smoke, burned hair, and sweat, making her gag.

Rusty lowered his head to the ground and coughed.

"Are you okay?" Wyatt joined them, running his hands over Rusty's body, checking for injury.

Jessica nodded. "I'm fine, but Rusty's coughing."

Wyatt examined the old horse. "He's breathed in a lot of smoke, Jessie. Just keep a close eye on him. We can call the vet if he gets too bad."

A loud bang issued from the front of the barn. Wyatt and Jessica turned in the direction of the sound.

"What was that?" Jessica stared at the front of the barn, trying to see what was going on.

Wyatt shrugged. "It sounded like a gunshot, but it could have been one of the gas containers in the barn exploding." He patted Rusty again, then pointed toward the pen. "Those horses we sold you are about to jump out of their hides. I'm going to let them out before one of them breaks a leg or the barn falls on them."

"B-but they don't have halters on," Jessica stammered. "We'll never catch them. They'll be out running on the range again." She thought of the little paint filly and how she'd never even gotten to know her.

"Well, that'll just give me, Dunce, and Gator something to do over the next few days," Wyatt said as he walked away. "Hey, how do you think we got them to your house in the first place?"

Rusty broke into another coughing fit and Jessica tried to comfort him. Wyatt opened the gate to the holding pen and stepped out of the way as the herd of young horses bolted away from the fire. The paint filly was one of the first horses to leave the enclosure. Jessica marveled at her speed as she flattened her little fox ears and sprinted away from the pandemonium, her well-muscled haunches propelling her at great speed. Jessica fleetingly wondered if she would ever see the beauty again. The horses were returning to the wild.

"Jessica!" Mrs. Warner called, rounding the corner of the burning building at a jog.

"I'm okay, Mom." She waved as her mother's shadowy figure moved across the illuminated backdrop of the fire. "How are Dad and Duncan?"

Mrs. Warner stopped to check Jessica and Rusty. "They're faring a lot better than this old horse." She clucked her tongue and ran her hands over Rusty's singed hide. "Better get him out of this smoke. The front yard is the best place for him. We had to put Duncan's horse down."

Jessica sucked in her breath. That explained the single blast of gunfire. She picked up the lead rope and asked Rusty to follow her. The old horse took several steps, then stopped to cough and wheeze. Jessica put a comforting hand on his neck and encouraged him to keep walking. She had to get him to a safe place where he could breathe easier.

Rusty continued to cough and she felt an iron band squeezing her chest. Rusty was her very first horse. She knew she would soon have to retire him for riding, but she'd never thought about him dying. She had to keep Rusty safe. She wouldn't let him suffer the same fate as her brother's horse.

Rusty made it to the front yard before stumbling and dropping to his knees. Jessica cried out, bending to help him up, but the old horse rolled onto his side and lay on the grass, sucking in great gulps of air as he continued to wheeze and blow through his nostrils. Even the loud crash of the barn falling to the ground in a shower of sparks couldn't convince the old horse to rise.

"Give him a few minutes to rest and then try to get him up," Mr. Warner said. "I don't want to have to put another one down tonight."

Jessica's heart tumbled. She couldn't let that happen. She sat on the ground and took Rusty's head in her lap, wiping her eyes with her sleeve and speaking words of comfort to him. The lump in her throat threatened to choke her as she swallowed a sob and laid her cheek on Rusty's neck. She'd give him a little while longer to rest, but then he had to get up. She knew he'd do it for her. She took a deep steadying breath. What was she going to do if he didn't pull through?

She gave up trying to be brave. The night had taken its toll. Jessica let the tears flow freely down her cheeks while she listened to Rusty's ragged breath move in and out of his lungs.

After a while Jessica sniffed and stared at the ruins of the burning barn with its lost supply of winter feed. Her eyes traveled to the still form of Duncan's horse. Their mother said that things always looked better by daylight. But this time it wouldn't matter how brightly the sun shone tomorrow. This disaster wouldn't ever look any better.

FOUR

Jessica woke with a start. She blinked at the bright light flooding the room, making her momentarily disoriented. The big-engine growl of her father's tractor hummed in the distance, drawing her further toward full consciousness. Turning her head, she spotted the smear of soot on her white pillowcase and inhaled the strong smell of smoke that still clung to her hair.

Memories of the previous night stampeded through Jessica's mind. She jumped from the bed, pulling back the blue curtains. Her stomach tightened when she saw her father operating the tractor with the scoop attached. He was digging a hole in the south field.

Jessica dropped the curtains back into place. She knew what that meant. There were already two horses, three cats, and a dog buried in that field. The new hole was for Duncan's horse. And maybe poor Rusty, too. But he had stood up last night and even walked a bit—enough to convince her dad to give him a chance.

She got out of bed and reached for a clean pair of jeans

and shirt, tossing the dirty, smoke-filled clothes from last night's catastrophe into the laundry basket. The firefighters had stayed to make sure there were no flare-ups from any hotspots they might have missed. The last fire truck had pulled out just before dawn. The barn was totally gone now, but at least their house had been saved. She pulled boots onto her bare feet, not wanting to waste time with socks. She had to check on Rusty right away.

Jessica pushed open the front door, startling her mother who stood on the walkway. "Is... is Rusty...?" she stammered, not wanting to say the words she feared might be true.

Mrs. Warner smiled in sympathy. "Rusty is still with us, Jess." She tucked a lock of her daughter's hair behind her ears and smiled encouragingly. "Marybeth called this morning, but you were sleeping so soundly, I didn't want to wake you."

Jessica nodded. "I'll call her later. Right now I've got to see how Rusty's doing."

"The vet is coming to check him," her mother said. "Your poor horse inhaled a lot of smoke last night, and he's still coughing and wheezing, but he's up and walking about a bit. Your father's afraid he might have singed his lungs."

Jessica tried not to panic, but she knew that could be a serious problem, even for a young horse. At Rusty's advanced age, it could prove fatal. "I'll go wait for Dr. Altom," she volunteered and hurried out to the corrals.

Jessica stopped in her tracks when she rounded the corner of the house and was hit by the full impact of the burned-out barn in broad daylight. What had once been a beautiful two-story wooden structure was now little more than blackened ashes and fragments of charred boards. She wrinkled her nose at the lingering scent of the fire and wondered how long it would be before the awful smell would go away.

A soft nicker drew her attention to the front corrals. "Rusty!" Jessica ran to her horse, throwing her arms around his neck and burying her face in his ragged mane. "I'm so glad you're all right."

She closed her eyes, feeling a hot trail of tears course down her cheeks. The familiar smell of Rusty was marred by the acrid odor of smoke and burned hair. She lifted her head and ran her hands over his body. Last night, in all the confusion, it had been difficult to tell just how injured her gelding was, but in the full light of day, Jessica could see the marks the live ash had seared into his coat.

In the distance, the tractor engine hummed, reminding her that Duncan's gelding hadn't fared as well as Rusty. She ached for her brother and his horse, but she was glad Rusty had been spared.

She scratched the old gelding behind the ears and straightened his forelock, looking into his kind brown eyes. "I'm so sorry this happened to you," she told him. "If you'd been in the front corral here, you wouldn't have been in danger."

Rusty nuzzled her cheek as if he understood her sadness. Jessica heard the rasping of his lungs as he whuffed soft breaths across her face. Another pang of guilt washed over her. If only she'd left him in the front corral! But she had done what she thought best for Rusty at the time. Her father and Duncan had put their horses in the barn, too. No one had expected a fire!

She cupped Rusty's muzzle in her hands and planted a kiss in the center of his whiskered nose. It made no sense to cry over what had happened. It wouldn't help Rusty get better. Right now she needed to concentrate on helping him.

Jessica rubbed Rusty's withers. He flicked his tail and bobbed his head, letting her know she'd hit a particularly sore spot. "Don't worry, ol' boy," she assured him. "The vet will be here soon and he'll make you all better."

But Rusty wheezed again, and Jessica wondered if she'd be able to keep her promise to her old friend. Would Dr. Altom be able to help the gelding?

The crunch of tires on the gravel driveway signaled the vet's arrival. Jessica stood on her toes to see over Rusty's back. She smiled and waved at Dr. Altom as he parked his truck in front of Rusty's corral.

"Guess you had a little excitement around here last night," the vet said, stepping from his truck and walking to the back to open the doors of his medical supply unit. He glanced at the area where the barn once stood and shook his head.

"Just a little," Jessica said with a weak smile. She liked Dr. Altom's sense of humor. He could lighten the mood of almost any bad situation. She watched him run his hands over Rusty, feeling the places where the sparks from the fire had burned his coat.

The vet pushed his wire-framed glasses up further on his nose and put the stethoscope to Rusty's girth, checking his heart and lungs. He listened at several different areas of the horse's body so he could get a complete diagnosis. After several minutes of examination, he pulled the stethoscope from his ears and pursed his lips.

Jessica didn't like the way the vet's brows drew together as he frowned. "What is it?" she asked in alarm.

Dr. Altom patted the old horse on the hip. "It's nothing we can't take care of," he said. "It's just that..." He paused and gazed off toward the nearby sagebrush-covered hills, then looked her straight in the eye. "Jessie, your dad's been hinting at getting you a new horse for a while now."

"But I don't want a new horse!" Jessica said in defense of her old friend. She pushed aside thoughts of the new paint filly, wanting to remain loyal to Rusty.

The vet walked to Jessica's side and leaned against the fence. "Rusty's been a good horse for you all these years, Jess. He made a great first horse for you to learn to ride on."

"But he's only twenty-two," Jessica countered, feeling the tears begin to burn the backs of her eyes. "Lots of horses can be ridden for years past that age."

"And some horses don't even make it to twenty-two." Dr. Altom shook his head and sighed. "Jessie, twenty-two is probably the youngest Rusty could be. Once a horse gets to the top of his years, it's a lot more difficult to read their teeth and determine exactly how old they are. Your parents had only a vague idea of Rusty's age when they bought him. He could be as old as twenty-eight." The vet paused. "And now he's got serious problems."

Jessica flinched. "How bad is he, Doc?"

The vet placed a boot on the fence and turned to look at Rusty. "He's got some serious damage to his lungs. I'm going to give him a steroid to help with any swelling he might have, and you'll have to keep him on a regular dose of antibiotics for a while. He should heal, but you won't be doing him any favors by riding him." He placed a fatherly arm around her shoulder. "It's time to retire the ol' boy, Jess."

Jessica choked back a sob. "He won't have to be put to sleep, will he?" She looked pleadingly at the vet. She could handle not being able to ride Rusty because of his health, but she'd miss him terribly if he had to be destroyed.

Dr. Altom smiled. "No, Jess. Just retire him out to pasture with your cows. You can feed him carrots every day and watch him be fat and happy. Consider it his reward for all those years of taking good care of you."

Jessica took a steadying breath. She would miss riding Rusty, but at least he'd still be around.

Her father joined them, sweeping his hat from his head and wiping a sleeve across his sweating brow. "Duncan's horse is taken care of. Please tell me we don't have to do the same for this animal."

Dr. Altom gave Mr. Warner a good-natured slap on the back. "I was just telling Jessie here that it's about time you made good on your promise to get her a younger horse. This ol' boy will live, but he won't be fit for riding anymore."

Her father stroked his mustache. "Well, we might have to put the new horse off for a little while, Jess. Our first priority's got to be getting that barn back up and restocking our winter feed supply."

Jessica nodded. At the moment, she didn't feel much like riding any horse but Rusty.

Mr. Warner nodded toward the corrals at the other end of the barnyard. The pens had small lean-to sheds that opened into the big front pasture. Several ranch horses grazed on the sparse grass in the fields. They hadn't been in any danger from last night's fire.

"We've still got a couple of old ranch horses you can ride," her father said. "Duncan's in the house getting ready to go round up the young ones. He's taking Grizz." He paused for a moment and smiled. "After this trip, that old bay ought to be ridden down enough for you to handle."

Jessica frowned. *Grizz* was short for Grizzly, and he pretty much lived up to his name. Being part quarter horse and part draft with a dash of Arabian made him a very large horse with a very large attitude. The big bay couldn't be beat as a cow-horse, but if a rider's attention dropped even a smidgen, he would find himself on the ground watching Grizz's hindquarters disappear over the ridge as the animal hightailed it back to the barn. Jessica didn't trust the unpredictable horse. She had to admit that he scared her.

Maybe it would be best to just wait and see what happened. Besides, she didn't want to jump right into getting a new horse. She'd spend the next few weeks helping Rusty get better. Maybe after that she'd feel like picking a new mount.

"Gator and Wyatt'll be here soon to round up those horses," her father said. "Could you help your brother out and catch Grizz for him? I'll finish up with Rusty. You don't like watching him get shots anyway."

Jessica took the halter and bucket of grain from her father. She hoped the brown beast would fall for the grain trick. Grizz hated being caught. He knew a halter meant he had to go to work, so at the first sight of one, the cagey gelding took off to the opposite side of the pasture. Duncan could make him stand for haltering, but the horse never paid much attention to her. Jessica could think of many things she'd rather do than chase Grizz around the five-acre pasture, but her father had asked her to do it.

She spotted Grizz near the opening to one of the corrals. But true to his contrary nature, the crafty gelding gave her a dubious look and sauntered off toward the middle of the field.

"I've got grain..." Jessica said in a sing-song voice, shaking the grain bucket.

Grizz stopped and looked back over his shoulder, as if trying to decide whether eating the molasses and grain feed was worth the riding he'd get. Jessica shook the bucket again and continued to walk forward with the halter behind her back. The big bay waited until she was within five feet of him, then picked up his walk, moving just fast enough to keep ahead of her.

Jessica groaned in exasperation, but continued to trail the gelding. By now, the other two ranch horses in the pasture had heard the grain rattling in the bucket and came over to investigate.

Feeling sorry for the animals that were trailing behind her, lipping her shirt and begging for a treat, Jessica stopped and gave them each a small handful of the sweet feed. That got Grizz's attention immediately. He pinned his ears and chased off the other two geldings, but he still refused to come close enough for Jessica to halter him.

Jessica sat the bucket at her feet and crossed her arms. "If you think I'm just going to give this to you, you're wrong," she scolded. Grizz stood facing her with his ears pricked. Jessica picked up the bucket and held it out. The bay gelding took a few steps forward and stretched his neck toward the bucket, stealing a few oats before dodging out of range of the halter.

"That does it!" Jessica stamped her foot. "I'm not wasting any more time on you. I've got a sick horse to take care of that *likes* to be pampered. I don't need to be out here chasing a knothead like you around the pasture. Duncan can catch you himself!"

She turned on her heels and marched back to the gate. As she passed through Grizz's corral, she looked over her shoulder and noticed that the big horse was following at a safe distance.

Jessica smiled. "I'll outsmart you at your own game," she promised, sitting the grain bucket down next to Grizz's shelter. She walked out of the pen and hid behind the next shed. Peeking around the corner, she watched the wily gelding stop at the entrance to the corral, snorting as he looked around, expecting to see Jessica. He spotted the red bucket standing by itself and shuffled forward, sticking his muzzle deep into the bucket.

"Gotcha," Jessica whispered, stepping quickly toward the corral gate and banging it closed. Grizz stared at her, looking surprised he'd been caught. Jessica laughed and hung the halter on the gate. "This time *I* won, pal," she gloated. "Dunce can handle you from here."

Dr. Altom had finished with Rusty by the time she returned. He showed her the antibiotic pills and the salve for the horse's burned spots. Jessica thanked the vet, then gave Rusty a flake of hay and sat on the side of the manger to watch him eat. He didn't have much of an appetite, but he picked out the best pieces of dried grass and clover and chewed them slowly.

"Wow!"

Jessica heard Marybeth's awestruck voice all the way across the yard. She stood and waved to her neighbor as the younger girl trotted up on her Appaloosa pony, Daisy.

Marybeth dismounted, then took off her riding helmet and shook out her shoulder-length blonde hair. She wore jeans that looked new and an imitation silver belt buckle. The shirt she had on was way too big for her. She pointed to where the barn had stood. "That is totally amazing!"

"Yeah," Jessica said. "Pretty bad, huh?"

Marybeth wrinkled her nose. "It really smells. How can you stand it?" She led her pony over to Rusty's corral, eyeing him suspiciously. "Is he okay?"

Jessica shrugged. "Not really. The vet says that I can't ride him anymore. His lungs are weak, and he's old." Tears stung her eyes and she turned her head away so Marybeth wouldn't see.

"Don't cry, Jess." Marybeth stared through the boards, her voice suddenly full of concern.

Marybeth's plea made Jessica feel even worse. She sat on the edge of the feeder and covered her face with her hands. She heard the creak of the fence as Marybeth crawled over it, then dropped down beside her.

"It'll be okay, Jess." Marybeth patted her awkwardly on the back, then draped an arm around her shoulder and sat very still while Jessica cried.

After a while Jessica sniffed loudly and wiped her eyes on her sleeve. "Sorry I'm such a blubber-baby."

"It's okay," Marybeth assured her. "If I couldn't ride Daisy, I'd be really sad too." She climbed back over the fence and untied her horse from the rail. "Do you want to borrow my horse for a couple of days? Maybe it'll make you feel better."

The offer made Jessica want to cry again. "Thanks, but my dad is going to make me ride Grizz."

"Ohhh," Marybeth's eyes widened in disbelief. "Yikes."

Jessica nodded. "Yeah, it sounds like a pretty bad idea to me, too. I think I'll just wait a while and see if Rusty gets better." She wanted to tell Marybeth more about the paint filly, and her hope that her father might let her keep the beauty for a riding horse. But it made her feel disloyal to Rusty so she kept her mouth shut.

Marybeth would get a chance to see all the pretty horses once Duncan and the Lightfoot boys brought them home again. *If* they brought them home again. Maybe by then, she'd feel like talking about it.

Marybeth put her foot in the stirrup and swung her leg over the saddle. "My mom told me not to be gone long. I just wanted to see you and find out how bad the fire was." She paused, looking at the burned out remains of the barn. "It looks *really* bad."

Jessica nodded in agreement. They sat there in silence for another moment. She hoped that Marybeth wouldn't say anything more. She didn't feel like talking about it. All she wanted to do was go to her room and get into bed and pretend that none of this had ever happened. Thankfully, Marybeth just waved and turned her horse for home.

Jessica stood and dusted off her pants. The barn was gone, along with a large portion of their winter's hay. Duncan's horse was dead, Rusty was sick and might not get better, and all of the new horses were running loose.

How could things get any worse?

FIVE

Mr. Warner was on the telephone in the kitchen when Jessica entered the house. She could hear him speaking in a businesslike tone.

She walked past him and flopped on the couch in the living room, resting her head on the small throw pillow. She could still hear her father's voice. She couldn't really make out his words, but she couldn't help noticing that he sounded rather irritated. A minute later, he abruptly hung up the phone. The sound of his boot heels echoed across the wooden floor of the kitchen as he walked toward the living room.

Jessica stared at her father as he stood in the doorway, running a hand over his worried face. He didn't seem to have noticed that she was there. It seemed strange to catch her father in an unguarded moment and see the worry lines etched in his strong features. She cleared her throat to let him know she was there.

"Have you been in here long?" Mr. Warner asked.

Jessica shook her head. "Only a minute. I'm kind of tired. I think I'll take a nap."

Her father managed a small smile. "You'll have to wait a minute for that nap. Can you go get your mother, Jessie? I'll call Duncan. I've something I want to discuss with everyone before your brother leaves to round up those horses."

Jessica hopped off the couch and went in search of her mother. She had a funny feeling in the pit of her stomach that the news, whatever it was, wouldn't be good. She found her mother by the burned barn, rummaging through the ashes.

Mrs. Warner lifted a charred piece of leather and tossed it on the grass. "That's what's left of the saddles," she said in disgust. "We've got some older ones that we stored in the bunkhouse, but all the good tack was in the barn." She looked around and sighed. "And now it's all gone."

Jessica could hear the tears in her mother's voice. She wanted to run over and give her a big hug, but it would probably just send them both into another crying fit. They didn't need that now. "Dad wants to see all of us up at the house before Duncan leaves," she told her mother.

Mrs. Warner nodded. "Your father was on the phone to the banks and the insurance company. Maybe he's got good news," she said.

Jessica didn't have the heart to tell her mother that her father's discussion on the phone hadn't sounded very encouraging. She followed her mother to the house and took her place at the kitchen table.

Everyone stared at Mr. Warner as he sat in his chair. Jessica thought he looked tired, and suddenly older.

"All right," Mr. Warner began. "I've never been one for

wasting words, so I'm just going to come right out and say this." He crossed his arms and looked down. "We're in a bit of a bind, folks. The insurance we had on the barn wasn't enough to cover the cost of rebuilding it. We didn't have the feed supply insured at all, and they'll only cover the cost of part of the tack and equipment." He took a deep breath and continued. "Cattle prices are down, and feed and grazing permits are up. We don't have enough money to cover all of our losses."

"What are we going to do?" Mrs. Warner asked. "We've got to have that barn built and the feed restocked before winter. We've got two hundred head of cows and calves. They won't have enough forage on that land to make it to auction in the fall, let alone through a tough winter."

Jessica quickly cut her eyes to Duncan, trying to gauge his reaction. But as usual, Duncan sat stoically in his chair, waiting until he had all the information before offering an opinion. She wished she had his patience. At the moment, what she really wanted to do was stomp her feet and scream at the top of her lungs, but she took her brother's cue and sat there quietly.

Mr. Warner reached for his wife's hand and gave it a gentle squeeze. "Don't worry, Kate, we'll come up with something. The insurance money will be here in a few days. We should have enough to get the barn halfway finished. We'll have to find a way to get the rest of it done. We're just going to have to buckle our belts and watch our spending."

He turned to Duncan. "Son, make sure you find those new horses, all fifteen of them. The money we get from breaking and selling them will put a lot of hay in the barn. If we don't restock that hay supply, those cows will be in a lot of trouble, and their sale is what puts food on our table."

Jessica frowned at the mention of the new horses. The pretty little filly would be sold. There would be no chance now for her to ask for the paint. Her family needed the money. End of story.

"What about mortgaging the property?" Mrs. Warner suggested. "We've got enough in equity to take out a good-sized loan."

Jessica thought her father was going to turn purple at the suggestion. She waited for the explosion, but he just took a deep steadying breath and spoke in a calm voice.

"I will not mortgage this land, Kate," Mr. Warner said. "That's what cost old man Smith his property last year. He got so far down, he couldn't make his payments and they took his land. I won't chance that." He looked at each of them around the table. "Don't worry. We'll rebuild and restock the barn by winter. You've got my word on that." A sense of uncertainty hung in the room like a wet horse blanket. Jessica felt as if her family was teetering on the edge of destruction, hoping for a big dose of luck to see them through.

"May I be excused?" Jessica asked.

Her mother nodded. "Yes, but not for long. We've all got a lot of work ahead of us today. I'll give you ten minutes and then I want you to meet me outside."

Jessica slid her chair back from the table. So much for taking a nap and hiding in bed the rest of the day. So many things had happened since last night. It seemed like her whole world had tipped on its end.

Just yesterday she'd been making big plans for the summer, which included finding a way to keep the paint filly for herself and having a great time riding Rusty through the desert. But now everything had changed.

She stepped out the back door just as the Lightfoot boys rode up.

"No worries, Jess," Gator called over his shoulder as he turned toward the hitching post. "We'll bring every one of those horses back."

Wyatt rode past Jessica, tipping his hat and giving her another one of his shy smiles. He nudged his horse into a canter to catch up with his brother. Jessica marveled at the way he sat his horse. Like Duncan and Gator, he moved with his mount. There was no extra bouncing on the saddle or kiltering off to one side. He looked a part of the horse.

Mrs. Warner waved to the Paiute boys. "Duncan will be down in just a minute," she called.

"Come on, Jess." Her mother steered her in the direction of what used to be their barn. "We've got to start cleaning up. Your father's digging holes with the tractor so we'll have a place to put those burned boards and debris. It's our job to fill the holes."

"Okay." Jessica pulled on a pair of heavy gloves and grabbed the wheelbarrow. While her father operated the tractor, moving the larger pieces of burned wood to the holes, she and her mom spent the entire afternoon hauling wheelbarrow loads of charred rubble. Shep ran back and forth between them all, inspecting each load that was dumped. The sickening smell of burned wood and smoldering hay filled Jessica's nostrils, making her want to gag. She found a kerchief and tied it over her nose, but it didn't help much.

By sundown, everyone was exhausted. Nobody felt like cooking over a hot stove, so their late-night dinner consisted of sandwiches and potato chips. Jessica was so worn out and sick to her stomach, she could only manage half a sandwich before she excused herself to go give Rusty his medicine and turn in for the night.

Even getting ready for bed was difficult. Her arms ached so badly from pushing the heavy wheelbarrow that she could hardly lift them. Just brushing her teeth and putting on her pajamas was a real pain.

She said good night to her parents, then climbed into her soft bed. She lay awake for a while, thinking and listening to the sounds outside her window. A lone cricket chirped in the night, and she could hear one of the horses nicker softly in the front pen. A pack of coyotes howled in the distance, calling to each other from the mountain tops.

Jessica thought of Duncan and the Lightfoot boys sleeping under the stars. She wished she could have joined them. Rounding up the new horses had to be a gazillion times more fun than cleaning up after the fire.

Her eyes grew heavy and she soon drifted into a deep sleep, but some time after midnight, her growling stomach woke her, reminding her she hadn't eaten much during the day.

Jessica put her feet over the side of the bed, cringing at the soreness of her muscles. She gingerly put on her slippers and crept down the stairs to raid the refrigerator. When she reached the bottom of the steps, she stopped short, seeing a light in the kitchen. Nobody in the house stayed up this late. Maybe her parents had forgotten to turn off the light before they went to bed.

She tiptoed across the living room floor, then halted in the shadows when she spied her father sitting at the kitchen table. His shoulders were slumped, and he was rubbing his forehead as if it hurt. He was so deep in thought he hadn't heard her come down the stairs, and she felt uncomfortable about catching him in another unguarded moment. In the soft light of the kitchen, Jessica was shocked to see that the man who had always seemed so strong and capable now looked so old and tired. Her heart ached for him.

She turned to leave, but not before she caught a glimpse of what her father was studying on the table. There before him, lined up in neat order, were the business cards the travel agents had left each time they came to call.

Jessica drew back. Was her father really considering taking them up on their offers? He'd been dead set against turning Wild Hawk Ranch into a guest ranch for city folk. Confused, she turned and crept back up the stairs, seeking the comfort of her bed.

She crawled under the covers and lay staring into the darkness of her room. The whole family knew how her father felt about renting their home out to strangers. If he would even consider such a thing, they had to be in even more trouble than she'd thought.

SIX

Jessica saw the dust cloud rising over the mountain before the riders and the herd came into view. She turned and shouted to her parents. "They're coming!" She'd spent the last hour preparing the pen, making sure the water tanks were topped off and the mangers were full of the sweet-smelling grass hay that several of the local ranches had donated to help out. The horses would be tired and thirsty after the long trek back to the ranch. She wanted them to be glad they'd returned. They needed to see Wild Hawk Ranch as their home.

Rusty pricked his ears and neighed a welcome to the returning horses as they picked their way down the mountain. Jessica was happy to see him perk up. That meant he had to be feeling better. She joined the old gelding in his corral and watched the approaching horses and riders. Squinting into the morning sun, she scouted for the black-and-white coat pattern of her favorite filly.

"Do you see her, ol' boy?" Jessie scratched him behind the ears. Rusty nickered as if in reply, but Jessica knew he was just responding to the approaching herd. She searched the sea of bays and chestnuts, spotting the one gray and the blue roan in their midst, but not the paint. Where was the filly?

She waited until the herd trotted into their pen, then went to join the boys. "Duncan, where's the paint filly?" She tried to keep the concern out of her voice, but she could tell by her brother's smile that he saw right through her. Later, when he decided it was time to talk, he'd probably lecture her about not falling in love with a horse they were going to sell.

He nodded his head toward the mountain. She shaded her eyes from the sun and saw the lone horse hobbling down the hillside trail. "What happened?" she cried in alarm.

Wyatt rode up beside her and dismounted. He towered over Jessie by six inches. When he smiled down at her, it made her stomach do a funny little flip. She cleared her throat nervously and took a step backwards, waiting for him to speak.

"Your little filly hurt her foot about five miles back," he said as he led his horse to the water trough. "She couldn't keep up with the herd, but we made sure she stayed within sight. You might want to walk Rusty out there and see if she'll follow him into the corral. That'd be a big help. She'll need to be kept apart from the others for a few days."

Her little filly? Was she that easy to read? Jessica glanced around for her father. She didn't want him to have any idea how much she liked the paint horse. All she'd get was a lecture. She already expected one from Duncan. Her chances of owning the beautiful horse had gone up in smoke the moment the lightning struck.

Jessica grabbed Rusty's halter from the rail of his corral and slipped it over his head. She had to stand on her toes to buckle it because the gelding held his head high, keeping his eye on the lone horse making its way down the trail. "Come on, pal." She tugged on the lead rope and led him through the gate. Let's give your new friend an escort back to the ranch."

Rusty walked at her side, his head bobbing as he eagerly drew closer to the black-and-white filly. Jessica kept the pace slow. Doctor Altom had told her to take him for slow, short walks, but cautioned her not to stress his damaged lungs. Already, she could hear the horse's breathing grow heavy and they hadn't even left the stable yard.

They walked another hundred yards and Jessica stopped near the sagebrush line. "We'll stop right here and wait for her," she said. Rusty dropped his head and cropped a small tuft of desert grass at their feet. "Eat now, while it's still green," she told him as she let Rusty pull her along to the next bunch of greenery. "As hot as it's getting, it won't be long before it'll all be dried up and yellow."

It always amazed her that the high desert could be so green at the start of summer, and yet within six to eight weeks would take on the muted gold and tan colors of a drought-ridden state. It wouldn't be long before her father would take their cattle to the high mountain pastures nearby. Without that rich mountain grass, they'd have a tough time putting weight on the calves before they sent them to market.

Jessica watched the filly pick her way gingerly down the path, remembering the mad dash the paint had made into the lightning-filled hills the night the barn burned just a few days ago. "I think I'll call you Storm Chaser," she said when the horse came within earshot. "Chase for short."

At the sound of her voice, Storm Chaser pricked her ears and stared at her with intelligent eyes. Jessica's heart melted. Chase was the most beautiful horse they'd ever had on this ranch. She reached over to rub Rusty's neck. Not that she didn't love Rusty with all her heart. All horses had their own beauty, but the gelding didn't have the conformation of a purebred, and his coat was plain.

Chase's short, well-shaped head and her broad chest and hindquarters showed her quarter horse ancestry. A paint horse could only be registered with the American Paint Horse Registry if it had quarter horse or Thoroughbred lineage. If there were any other breed in the line, it had to go to the Pinto Registry.

The filly stopped twenty feet from where they stood. Rusty nickered a warm welcome and Chase returned the gesture. Jessica tugged on the gelding's halter. "Let's show her the way home, old man."

Her father was the only one left in the stable yard when they returned. He watched their approach, and Jessica knew he was assessing the filly's limp, trying to determine how badly she'd injured it.

"Let her follow Rusty into his pen," her father said.

Jessica smiled. It made sense that the two horses needing care would be put in the same pen—and they just happened to be her two favorite horses on the ranch. Chase seemed at ease with Rusty, and it would certainly make it easier for Jessica to get acquainted with the pretty paint.

Her dad opened the gate to the corral and waited for them to enter. "She seems to like the old guy, and he's definitely taken a shine to her," he said. "Rusty's calm influence will help in getting this filly gentled, and maybe the company will give Rusty something to live for."

Jessica wanted to shout with joy. Now would be the perfect time to ask her father again about training. She removed the halter from Rusty's head and turned back to face her father. "Um, Dad, since Storm Chaser is going to be sharing a pen with Rusty, would it be okay if I started working with her?"

Jessica cringed inside as soon as the paint's new name escaped her lips. She drew a deep breath, watching the way her father's eyes narrowed. He'd warned her a million times not to name the new horses or get too attached to them. Jessica crossed her fingers, praying he'd ignore her slip-up and say yes to the training.

"Jess, I know you mean well, honey..."

He might as well have put his thoughts in neon lights over his head. She knew what was coming next.

"I still think you're a little too young to start breaking horses," her father continued.

"But Duncan was younger than I am right now when he started." She crossed her arms over her chest and frowned.

Her father removed his hat and slapped it across his leg. "But Duncan was bigger and stronger. He's, well, a..."

"A boy?" Jessie finished the words for her father. It cut her to the quick to know he thought that way. She could train a horse just as well as any stupid boy if her father would only give her a chance. "You're not being fair," she said. Her voice came out ragged as she fought against her anger.

"That's not what I meant, Jessica Lynn. You have to be good and strong to be able to handle these unbroke animals." He plopped the hat back on his head, snugging it down like he expected a storm.

Jessica knew the argument was over. Her father only used her middle name when he was at the end of his patience.

"You can try to get the halter on that filly, and I'll be grateful if you do," he said, in a voice that brooked no argument. "But the breaking will be left to Duncan. Maybe we'll get you started next season when you've got a little more meat on your bones, Jess."

Jessica watched her father walk away. There was a sadness in his face when he turned and left. She knew it pained him to say no, but he'd done it just the same.

She turned back to the horse pen, the halter still in her hand. "I don't supposed you'd let me walk up and put this on you?" she said to Storm Chaser. The paint cocked her ears at the sound of Jessica's voice, but she maneuvered to stand behind Rusty, keeping a safe distance from Jessica. She moved as if her foot pained her terribly. Jess knew they needed to get Chase gentled quickly so they could treat her hoof.

She dug into her pocket, pulling out the carrot she'd stashed there before coming down to prepare the pen. She snapped it in half, and Rusty immediately recognized the sound. He stepped forward boldly, leaving the paint to fend for herself while he munched happily on the treat.

"You could have one too, you know." She bit off a smaller piece and offered it to Chase in the flat of her hand.

The little horse sniffed the air, her nostrils widening as

she tried to take in the scent. Jessica moved forward one step, holding her breath and praying that she could get close enough for the filly to take the tidbit out of her hand. Chase stood still through one more footstep, then retreated to a safe distance, eyeing her warily.

Jessica's shoulders slumped. Maybe her father was right. Maybe she needed to wait one more year before she took up training horses. How could she train Chase when she couldn't even get a halter on her?

"You were handled by people once," she told Chase. "Don't you remember? You were brought into the Lightfoots' barn at five months old with the rest of the colts and fillies and handled for the rest of the winter. Then they turned all of you out to the desert for a couple of years to play and grow." She sighed. "I guess you forgot everything about people when you were out in the wild. I've got to help you remember what it was like when you trusted humans. You're three years old now. It's time for you to learn to carry a rider."

She grabbed the stiff-bristled brush from the bucket outside the corral and ran it over Rusty's coat, whisking the dirt and loose hairs away with a flick of her wrist. Chase remained on the other side of the gelding. If Jessica stood on her toes and stretched across Rusty's back, she could reach the filly's shoulder with the brush.

At first, Storm Chaser startled at the touch of the grooming tool, but after a few more strokes, she stood still, her lips twitching in appreciation. The paint probably thought it was Rusty giving her a scratch. Jessica leaned a little further over

Rusty's back, trying to reach more of Chase, but when the filly saw her arm move, she stepped nervously to the rail and stayed out of reach.

Duncan appeared outside the corral. Jessica was surprised to see him. She hadn't heard him approach. "She doesn't want me to touch her," Jessica said with a frown as she tossed the brush back into the bucket.

"Give it some time," Duncan suggested. "She's been wild for the last couple of years. It doesn't happen all in one day."

Jessica didn't care. She wanted it to happen *now.* They needed to look at that injured hoof before infection set in. "So what should I do?"

"You've got Rusty to help you," Duncan said. "A lot of the time these young horses take their cues from the older ones. They look to see how the older horse reacts to a situation and they act the same way."

"Gee, thanks!" Jessica called after Duncan's retreating form.

Duncan looked back over his shoulder. "You'll figure it out, Jess."

Jessica knew she wouldn't get any more out of Duncan right now. He'd said plenty. She'd have to sort this one out on her own. She leaned her elbows on the fence and observed the two horses for a while. Sure enough, everywhere Rusty went, Storm Chaser followed like a little puppy. The filly limped along behind him, walking when he walked, stopping when he stopped. The paint watched Rusty drink from the water trough and sidled up beside him, sticking her muzzle deep into the trough.

An idea suddenly occurred to Jessica. She knew her father and brother would recommend soaking the hoof to draw out any infection. She quickly ran to the tool shed and dragged a couple of old wooden saw horses over to Rusty's feeder, blocking off the sides so the horses would have to stand directly in front of the feeder to eat.

Next she went to the old pig pen and found the rectangular feeder they used for the weaner pigs they'd raised last season. The feeder was long and shallow. It would work perfectly for soaking the foot of a reluctant horse. After washing the container thoroughly, Jessica lugged several buckets of warm water from the house and gathered some Epsom salts and vinegar. She'd watched her father use these ingredients before. They worked together to draw the infection out of a wound.

Rusty watched calmly, but Storm Chaser snorted in surprise as Jessica brought the metal pig feeder into the corral and placed it in front of the manger where the horses ate. Next, she poured in the warm water and added the Epsom salts and vinegar.

Rusty stepped forward and sniffed the strange concoction, lifting his upper lip and making a funny horse face. "I know it stinks," Jessica told him with a laugh. "Like my dad always says, 'The worse it smells, the better the medicine.'"

Chase stood far back from the odd-smelling brew. Jessica hoped her plan would work. She went to the hay pile and grabbed a big armload of hay. Rusty saw her coming and nickered in excitement. He loved to eat.

Jessica tossed the hay into the feeder and stepped back to

see if the horses would venture into the water to get to the food. Rusty gave the pig feeder a suspicious look and lowered his head to sniff the water. He stood for several moments, pondering the situation.

"Come on, Rusty," she pleaded. "I'm counting on you."

The old gelding put one foot in the water and snorted. Jessica was sure he was going to turn and run for the other end of the pen, but his belly got the better of him. He put both feet in the pig feeder and stretched his neck toward the manger full of grass hay.

Chase wandered closer. Jessica noticed that when the filly stood still, she shifted the weight off her hurt foot. Her injury seemed to be getting worse. After a few minutes of assessing the situation, the paint apparently realized that Rusty was eating all the good stuff. She hobbled to within a few feet of the hay.

Jessica had to put her hand over her mouth to keep from laughing as Chase contorted her body this way and that, trying to get to the hay without stepping into the water. Rusty continued to munch away, turning his head now and then to look at the filly.

Finally, Storm Chaser could stand it no longer and stuck one foot into the water. Jessie was glad Rusty had his two front feet and most of his weight planted in the pig feeder, because Chase snorted loudly and pulled her foot out of the water with such force, it would have upset the entire thing if Rusty hadn't been standing in it.

"Come on, Chase, you can do this," Jessica said encouragingly as the little paint moved forward and sniffed the water.

This time when she stuck a foot in, she pawed at the metal feeder, sending water all over herself and Rusty. She played around for a few more moments, trying to figure it out. Then she took her cue from the calm old gelding and lowered her injured foot gingerly into the water, pushing her muzzle into the hay.

"That's my girl!" Jessie crowed, but not loud enough to spook the filly. She hoped she'd put enough hay in the feeder to keep the horses standing still for at least another half-hour. That would go a long way to helping Chase's foot.

Jessica sat on a bucket outside the fence and watched the horses eat. From time to time Rusty would poke his nose at the filly, letting her know he was boss. "Be a gentleman," Jessica scolded. "She's your guest."

"Hey, Jess!" Duncan called as he came up behind her. He stopped and looked at the two horses standing in the container of water. "Whew!" he said, wrinkling his nose. "Smells like Dad's drawing liniment."

Jessica smiled. "Maybe."

Duncan tousled her hair. "Pretty smart. Dad will be impressed that you came up with that one."

Jessica couldn't help but feel proud. It felt good to do something right for a change. Her father and brother seemed to come by their horse knowledge naturally, but it was a whole lot harder for her.

Duncan nodded toward the house. "Dinner is ready a little early. Dad wants to have another one of his family meetings. Why don't you toss another flake of hay into the feeder so that filly can soak her foot a little longer?"

Jessica placed a flake of hay in the feeder from Rusty's side, being careful not to startle the younger horse. "I'll be back later," she promised, then turned and followed Duncan back to the house.

She wondered what her father would have to say this time. "Please let it be something good," she whispered to herself as she climbed the back steps. At this point, she didn't think her family could take another slam of bad news.

SEVEN

Jessica took her cue from the somber look on her father's face. She slipped quietly into her chair at the dinner table. Her dad needed to stop handing out bad news in the kitchen or they'd all end up with ulcers after every meal. She put her napkin in her lap and waited.

Her father picked up the platter of chicken and took two big pieces. Jess knew he was trying to act as if everything was normal, but she knew better. Things were *not* normal, and wouldn't be anytime soon.

As the food was being passed around, Mr. Warner began, "I'm sure everyone has noticed the travel agents who've paid us visits all year long?"

Duncan couldn't hide his grin. "Kind of hard to notice when you chase them off so quickly."

Jessica wasn't sure the mood was right for joking. She quickly took a bite of a chicken leg to stop herself from laughing.

The corner of her father's mouth turned up in a half-smile. "Well, all that's about to change soon." He glanced at his wife, who nodded encouragingly. "Your mother and I have decided to give the dude ranch idea a shot."

Jessica's mouth dropped open.

Her father continued, "Starting tomorrow, we're going to clean out the old bunk rooms and get them ready for guests. Wild Hawk Ranch is about to change."

Jessica wanted to jump from her chair and yell, *Yes!* but she sat tight. Beside her, Duncan frowned.

"We've got a lot of work to do, folks," her mother said.

"And we'll need something safe for the city slickers to ride," her father reminded them. "We can borrow a couple of gentle horses and tack from the Lightfoots to begin. I want to start small to make sure we can handle this. And find out if it's what we want."

Jessica took the salad bowl from Duncan and put two big scoops of mixed lettuce and a bunch of cherry tomatoes on her plate.

"According to one of the travel agents, some of the visitors may be real horsemen who are looking for someplace different to vacation with their animals. They'll bring all their horses and tack with them. It's the new 'in' thing to do," he said with a chuckle.

Jessica hoped that some of those visitors would be kids her own age. Summer vacation had barely started, and already she was lonely.

She thought about Marybeth and felt a small twinge of guilt. The younger girl considered Jessica her best friend. But Jessica couldn't help wishing for someone more her own age to be best friends with. The visitors would only be temporary guests, but it would be nice to have other kids around the ranch—especially if they were horse crazy like her.

Duncan cleared his throat and waited for their father's nod before he spoke. "We just lost our barn and hay supply. So..." He fiddled with his potatoes and stared down at his plate.

"Go on," Mrs. Warner encouraged. "What are your concerns, Duncan?"

"Can we afford to do this? I mean, I love Wild Hawk and all, but it's not exactly a five-star resort."

Jake Warner tipped back in his chair and laughed. It was the first time Jessica had heard him laugh since the fire.

Mrs. Warner shushed her husband and squeezed Duncan's hand. "We'll be cutting a few corners, honey, but we've got enough money to get the barn started and buy the towels and linens and things we'll need for the guests. A lot of the other stuff we've already got lying around here. It's mostly going to be a matter of getting everything together and putting in a lot of hard work."

Duncan went back to eating. That told Jessica that her brother thought everything would be fine. She stared around the table. Everyone seemed to be okay with the project. That meant they'd have guests at Wild Hawk soon!

Jessica could hardly wait to finish dinner. She wanted to get back to the corrals to check on Rusty and Chase, then maybe afterwards she'd give Marybeth a call. She was sure her friend would be pretty excited about the dude ranch, too. They'd talked many times when they'd ridden together, wishing that there were more girls nearby for them to hang out with.

When she finished her last bite of salad, Jessica excused herself so she could check on the horses. Her mother winked at her as she left the table, and Jessie realized that her mom probably felt the same way about the prospect of dude ranch guests as she did, even though it would mean a lot of extra work. She flashed her mother a smile and went outside.

Rusty nickered as soon as he saw her.

"You just finished eating, you old greedy-gut," Jessica told him. "Don't be asking for more. I'm just here to clean out the pan you guys were soaking your feet in."

Chase eyed her warily and snorted when Jessica dragged the metal pan to the edge of the corral. The water sloshed over the sides and was quickly absorbed into the dry ground. She dragged the container outside the railing and dumped it over, holding her breath as the smelly concoction spread across the sand.

She rinsed and stored the pan, then returned to the corral and sat on the top rail. Rusty walked forward and stuck his nose in her midsection, begging for a scratch. She played with his forelock, then scratched his neck and finger-combed his mane. From her perch atop the fence, Jess could plainly see the burn marks on Rusty's back. She climbed down and rummaged through the brush bucket, looking for the salve she had placed there.

Rusty stood patiently while she dabbed the medicine on his burned areas. Jessica knew some of them had to hurt badly, but the old horse stood patiently, letting her care for him. She glanced over his broad back, staring at Storm Chaser. "Do you see how this is done? See how nice and quiet Rusty stands here?" she chided. "You're supposed to act like I'm your friend."

Storm Chaser flicked her ears, listening to the sound of Jessica's voice. Jessica tried to keep her words soft and even, the way her father had taught her. A loud or excited tone of voice might cause a horse to think there was trouble. In the wild, a horse's best defense was to run away from the danger. Jessica didn't want the new filly to run away from her.

A movement on the other side of the stable yard caught her eye. Jessica stood on the rail to get a better view as Duncan entered the new horses' pen and singled out the blue roan. He expertly and quietly drove the gelding toward the opening to the next pen without causing the rest of the herd to move.

Jessie sighed. Her brother was a great horseman. Horses responded to Duncan like he was one of their own. If she'd gone into that pen, the new horses would have bolted every which way. Some day she hoped to be as good at working with the beautiful animals as her father and brother. But even her dad recognized Duncan was special. He had always had a way with horses.

"I'll be back," she said to Rusty and Chase as she climbed off the fence and tossed the ointment into the brush bucket. Duncan was starting work on the first of the new horses, the blue roan, and she wanted to watch. Maybe if she could learn how he did things, she'd be able to do a little work with Chase. If she could get the halter on the skittish filly, maybe her father would have more faith in her and let her try to train the paint.

Jessica hung back under the shade of the big quaking aspen trees not far from the training pen. She hoped Duncan wouldn't notice her. He didn't like having an audience.

At first, her brother didn't do anything. He just let the horse move around the circle, looking over the fence and calling to the other horses. Jessica recognized Rusty's and Chase's cries of concern along with the wild ones in the pen. The blue roan continued to pace on the side closest to his buddies. Being a herd animal, he wanted to get back to his friends.

Duncan let the colt pace for another minute, then coiled his lasso and gently urged the roan into trotting the entire circular pen. The colt tried to ignore him, but with each insolent toss of the horse's head, Duncan lifted the rope higher into the air or slapped it against his thigh, causing the colt to move a little bit faster.

Her brother preferred to work the young horses in the evening after dinner. It was cooler and he could push them harder. After a few minutes, the exercise began to wear on the colt. Jessica noticed that the blue roan looked inward to Duncan, recognizing that the boy was the one forcing him into running.

Jessie heard the crunch of boots and turned to see Marybeth walking toward her. Today Marybeth had on baby blue chaps over her jeans, a brightly colored western shirt, and a too-big hat that had to belong to her father. Jess wanted to roll her eyes, but instead she just smiled a welcome.

Marybeth started to speak, but Jessica put her finger to her lips, pointing to Duncan and the horse in the round pen.

Marybeth tiptoed the rest of the way and stopped beside her. Jessica could tell that her friend was wondering why they were being so secretive.

"Duncan doesn't like people watching him," Jessica whispered. "I thought I'd stand back here and spy. Maybe I can learn something."

Her friend nodded. "So you can work with that paint filly you e-mailed me about, right?"

Jessica shrugged. "If I can pick up some pointers, I can use them on any horse, not just Storm Chaser," she said.

"Why don't you just ask your brother to teach you some stuff?" Marybeth asked. "Duncan's really nice. I'm sure he'd do it."

Jessica shook her head. "The problem is, my father doesn't want me training horses. He thinks I'm too young." She crammed her hands deep into her jean pockets. "If he'd just give me a chance, I could prove to him that I'm ready."

"Oh," said Marybeth. "I get it."

Duncan took one step toward the colt and raised his rope. The roan slid to a halt and reversed direction in a perfect rollback on the fence, cantering off at a good clip and kicking up his heels.

"Wow," Marybeth whispered. "How'd he get him to do that?"

"I'm not sure." Jessica watched in fascination. "I'm trying to figure it out." Duncan hadn't said a word to the horse, or taken more than one step forward. Yet the colt seemed to read his mind and act on cue.

At that moment, Duncan turned in their direction, his gaze

seeming to penetrate the shadows of the large trees. Jessica and Marybeth both tried to duck.

"No sense hiding in the trees," Duncan said in a slow, easy voice. It sounded almost like the one he used on the skittish horses he trained. "Come on out here if you want to learn something."

Jessica grabbed Marybeth by the shirt and dragged her friend out with her. She didn't know why she was suddenly shy around her brother—probably because she knew he didn't like being spied on, and that was *exactly* what she'd been doing.

"You can come a little closer, but don't get too near the pen. I don't want this colt to get distracted."

The blue roan turned his attention on the girls as soon as they stepped out of the shadows. Duncan waved the rope and made smooching noises, pulling the colt's concentration back to him. The horse made several more rounds before Duncan took a step forward, raising the rope. The colt immediately changed direction.

"See what I'm doing here?" Duncan asked.

Marybeth didn't make a peep. She seemed a little bit intimidated by Duncan and his talent with horses. Jessica answered for the both of them. "Well, he's doing a nice rollback, sliding and turning on his haunches and jumping off in the other direction, but I don't know how you could have taught him that in just a few minutes. All you're doing is raising your rope."

Duncan smiled. "I'm using the horse's natural tendencies and abilities to get him to do what I want."

Jess nodded and stepped a little closer.

"When this horse first entered the pen, he ran around and kept pacing the side that his herd mates were on," Duncan continued. "All he was thinking about was how to get back to them. Then I asked him to trot for me." He smooched the horse into an extended trot. "See? I'm making him work and he's starting to get tired, so now he's paying attention to me, just like I want him to."

Duncan took a step toward the horse and raised his rope again. The stout quarter horse slid to a stop, spinning on his hind legs and charged off in the opposite direction. Then Duncan lowered his rope and let his arms drop to his sides. The colt halted and turned inward, facing him.

"Good boy," Duncan crooned. The horse's ears flicked forward and back, listening to the sound of the boy's voice. The roan dropped his head a little and licked his lips. "See that?" Duncan said. "That means he's thinking about what just happened. Good boy." He rewarded the horse with the soft sound of his voice.

Duncan turned and motioned for Jessica to enter the pen.

"Me?" she squeaked.

Her brother offered her a big smile. "You said you wanted to learn how to train horses, didn't you? Well, here's your first lesson."

Jessica looked over her shoulder toward the house. What would her father think? She knew he was mainly worried about her falling off and getting hurt. Free lunging a horse in the round pen wasn't riding, so her father couldn't really object to that. Could he?

"I'm not going to offer again," Duncan said.

Marybeth gave her a push and Jessica stumbled forward. She quickly squeezed through the rails before Duncan had a chance to change his mind—or her father came out of the house to object. She was going to get her first official training lesson!

EIGHT

Jessica walked to where Duncan waited in the middle of the pen. He pointed to a long lunge whip on the ground near her feet. "You can start out with that. It'll make things easier for you."

She picked up the whip, then stood in the center of the ring with her brother. The blue roan took his eyes off them and stuck his head over the top bar of the pen, calling to his friends.

"Get after him now," Duncan said. "Bring his attention right back here to us."

Jessica snapped the whip. At the sound of the sharp crack, the colt took off in a spray of sand, kicking up his heels as he circled the pen at a dizzying speed.

"Easy, there, big guy," Duncan said, turning in a circle while keeping his eye on the horse.

"How come you don't get dizzy?" Jessica asked.

"Just keep watching the colt," Duncan instructed. "If he starts to forget about us and looks anywhere but at you and me, just shake that whip and make him go faster. He needs to know that you're the boss."

Jessica kept her eye on the horse and nodded.

"You know how horses always have a pecking order?" Duncan said. "Well, right now you're trying to show him that you're the lead horse, and he has to do what you say."

When the roan slowed his pace, Jessica stepped forward and snapped the whip. The colt immediately came to a sliding halt and pivoted on his hind legs. Then he charged off in the other direction.

"What happened?" Jessica cried. "I asked him to speed up, but he turned and went the other way."

"Well, you actually asked him to turn," Duncan said.

"What do you mean?" Jessica asked, confused.

"Imagine that a horse has an invisible line leading from just in front of his withers and all the way to the ground."

Duncan motioned for Marybeth to come over, too. The younger girl squeezed eagerly through the steel railing. She looked thrilled to be included in the training session.

"Here's what happens," Duncan continued. "When you step toward the front end of the horse, or point the whip in front of that imaginary line, the horse will turn and go the other direction. If you put pressure from behind that line, it will cause the colt to move forward. Give it a try, Jess. Make him turn and go the other direction."

Jessica concentrated hard, trying to determine when to make her move. It was hard with the horse cantering at a fast pace.

"Come on, Jess," Marybeth said. "You can do it."

Jessica picked her moment, stepped forward, and shouted the word "turn," but the roan shied inward toward the rail and broke into a fast trot.

"Try it again," Duncan said.

Jessica tried, but once again, the horse dodged closer to the panels and continued in the same direction.

"You need to get more ahead of him," Marybeth shouted over the sound of the horse's heavy breathing and the pounding of hooves in deep sand.

"Great," Jessica muttered under her breath. Like she really needed a kid telling her how to do things. Marybeth might not find this so easy to do if she were doing it herself. "Why is it that you barely speak above a whisper and hardly move at all, and the horse knows exactly what you want? I practically yell, and almost step in front of him, and he still doesn't do what I want."

Duncan moved up behind Jessica and took her by the shoulders, steering her to the place where she needed to be. "It just takes time and patience to figure it all out," he said. "Sometimes you've got to start big to get it right and scale back later. Now, when I say go, step out and point that whip ahead of the horse. Make him believe that you're the one in charge."

Jessica nodded.

"*Go!*"

Jessie didn't hesitate this time. She stepped forward and pointed her whip at the horse's nose. "Turn!" she commanded. To her delight, the roan gelding slammed on the brakes and turned toward the fence in a perfect rollback.

"Let him circle a few times, then turn him back the other way," Duncan said, stepping away.

The gelding trotted three more rounds. When Jessica tried to turn him in the other direction, however, the horse ignored her once again.

"Watch your timing, Jess!" Duncan shouted.

Marybeth crept closer. "Now, Jess!" she yelled.

This time, Jessica didn't hesitate. She let the horse know exactly what she wanted him to do. He shifted all of his weight to his hindquarters and performed a perfect turn toward the fence line.

"Good job, Jess!" Duncan said.

"Woohoo!" Marybeth called, clapping loudly.

Jessica smiled big and basked in the glory of the moment. She was actually learning to train horses! As soon as Storm Chaser was sound, she'd be able to try this on the filly. Her father couldn't possibly get mad at her for improving the horse. She technically wouldn't be riding Chase, Jessica reasoned, so there wouldn't be any danger.

It just might happen. The next few days would be filled with cleaning and getting the bunkhouses ready for guests. Hopefully, in between chores and while her dad was busy on other things, she could find some time to soak the paint's foot and let it heal. If it got better soon, she might even have a chance to practice her new training skills on the little filly.

"Okay, Jess," Duncan said, interrupting her thoughts. "This time, go still and lower the whip to your side. We want this colt to stop his movement and turn in to face us."

"What makes you think he'll do that?" Jessica asked.

Duncan took back the whip and set it at their feet, motioning for Jessica to drop her hands to her sides. "Because he's tired and he wants to rest."

Just as Duncan had predicted, the roan slowed to a halt and turned in to face them. "Good boy," Duncan praised him, and the roan took a step toward them. Duncan turned to Jessica. "By this time tomorrow, I'll have a halter on him."

"Right," Jessie said, giving her brother a skeptical look.

"Wow," Marybeth said. "Really?"

Duncan grinned. "Guess you'll just have to show up tomorrow and see."

* * * * *

The next morning, Jessica sprang out of bed as soon as her alarm sounded. Today they'd begin cleaning the bunkhouses. She never thought she'd be excited about housework, but the sooner they got the buildings in order, the faster the guests would arrive—and the faster she'd have new friends!

Money for the ranch would arrive faster, too. Her father had said that the new hay crop would be ready to cut in another month—if they got another good rain. If they didn't, the hay wouldn't grow much and they'd have fewer bales on their next cutting. Her family needed a heavy crop to make up for what they'd lost, and they also had to put up as much as they regularly did on the second cutting.

Jessica sighed. It seemed that ranchers were always at the mercy of Mother Nature.

She slipped downstairs and poured herself a glass of orange juice, then fixed a quick bowl of cereal. Marybeth had helped her set out the cleaning buckets and brooms the night before. Now they were just waiting for someone to come along and use them.

"Good morning, Jess." Her mother kissed the top of her head and reached for the cereal box. "No time for making a hot breakfast this morning. We've got lots of work ahead of us." She smiled at Jessica as she poured milk over her cereal and picked up her spoon. "We received a check from the insurance company. Some of the lumber for the new barn will be delivered this morning. And we already have reservations for our first vacationers."

"It's going to take a while to build the barn," Jessica said. "If the vacationers bring horses, where are we going to put them?"

Mrs. Warner took a sip of her hot coffee. "Well, all of our corrals have covered shelters in them. We'll put our horses out in the pasture and let the guests' horses take the corrals. Mr. Williams down the road said he'd loan us a couple of his portable stalls. Besides," she added, "these first guests are getting their vacation package at a discounted rate. They'll just have to deal with the barn problem, same as us."

"So tell me about the visitors," Jessie said. "Are there any kids? How old are they? When do they get here?"

"Slow down, honey," Mrs. Warner said, raising her hands in the air as if to ward off all the questions. "I don't have many details, but it looks as if we'll have three families in the first bunch, and they'll stay for ten days. There are a total of seven kids and all of them are teenagers, I believe."

Jessica was too excited to finish her cereal. There were teenagers. And they'd be right here on Wild Hawk Ranch! They could ride horses all day, swim in the afternoon, and make s'mores around the campfire at night. Then she thought of something else. "Will we have enough horses?" she asked her mother.

"Some of the guests are bringing their own mounts." Mrs. Warner rinsed off the breakfast dishes and stacked them in the sink. "We've already contracted with the Lightfoots to use ten of their horses as we need them. We should be okay in that area."

She got out two pairs of work gloves and put them on the counter. "I guess we'd better figure out who you're going to be riding, Jess. We're planning to take the cattle up to the higher pastures while our visitors are here. We've got to get these calves fattened up so they bring the best price possible. You're going to need a dependable mount."

Jessica frowned. "I hope Dad doesn't say I have to ride Grizz. That horse is worse than a bear!"

Mrs. Warner laughed. "Grizz does have his moments, doesn't he?" she agreed. "But come on, Jess, let's get to work. The boys are out putting in stakes for the new barn, and our guests will be here in three weeks. It'll take us every bit of that time, maybe more, to get this place shaped up."

Jessica pulled on her boots and grabbed a pair of rubber gloves. No telling what kind of grime and iggly-squigglies they'd find in those two old bunkhouses. It had been years since they'd done anything with them besides use them for storage. She opened the back door and was surprised to find Marybeth sitting on the back stoop.

Marybeth jumped up, all smiles, and Jessie couldn't help but smile back. Her friend was wearing a pair of old bib overalls that were too big for her and had the pant legs rolled up several times. A pair of work gloves stuck out of her back pocket, and she held a broom in her hand.

"I know you didn't invite me, but I wanted to help," she said, giving Jess a look that begged to let her stay. "My mom said I could if it's okay with you."

"Fine with me," Jessica said. "Thanks." The more hands, the better, as far as she was concerned. It was sweet of Marybeth to want to help out. She wondered whether all the neighbors were talking about the trouble Wild Hawk Ranch was in, and whether this dude ranch thing would work out. She didn't even want to think about what might happen if their cattle didn't bring a good price at auction.

"So where do we start?" Marybeth asked.

"Well, I've got to feed Rusty and Chase first," Jessica said.

"Okay." Marybeth trotted after her friend as they headed to the corrals. "This is going to be fun today."

Fun? Jessica wondered. She doubted it, but if that's what Marybeth thought, she wouldn't disagree.

When they reached the corrals, Jessica dragged out the soaking tub, explained her plan, and showed Marybeth how to mix the water, salts, and vinegar to make the drawing agent for Chase's foot. She was glad to see the filly walking better this morning. This time, when she threw the hay in the feeder Chase only hesitated a moment before following Rusty into the tub.

Duncan walked by and nodded approvingly. Jessica couldn't help feeling proud. She'd taken the best care she could of the pretty filly. Then she quickly had to remind herself that Chase wasn't hers.

"Why are you frowning, Jess?" Marybeth asked.

"Oh, it's nothing." Jessie turned from the horses and led the way to the bunkhouses. For now she was going to pretend that Chase belonged to her, and she'd keep bugging her brother for more training lessons.

"Let's get started!" Mrs. Warner called from the cabins.

Jessica gave Rusty one last pat and headed toward her mom with Marybeth trailing behind.

"Do you want to do the honors, Jess?" Mrs. Warner waved her arm, indicating the door of the first bunkhouse.

Jessica grabbed the rusty old handle and gave it a turn, pushing against the rough grain of the wooden door. It swung inward with a loud groan, exposing the interior of the little-used building.

They all stared at the inside of the bunkhouse. After years of being used as a catch-all for all of their junk and building materials, it was a mess.

Jessica stepped through the door, batting at a spiderweb that drifted against her face. She hoped the spider wasn't crawling on her clothing now. She hated creepy crawly things.

Rows of boxes and various items that her mother had moved from the house over the years were piled throughout the forty-foot-long building. The bunks had been built back before her family owned Wild Hawk Ranch, when working cowboys had lived in them. There were no blankets on the beds and no pillows. No closets, no dividing walls, and no door on the bathroom.

Jessica wondered how all this would ever work. It would

cost a lot to buy linens and curtains and put up walls so each family could have a bit of privacy. For a moment, she felt guilty about wanting to keep Chase. Selling the filly would help pay for a lot of repairs to the ranch. And she knew her parents could find her an old horse that didn't cost as much as Chase would bring at auction. But it wouldn't be the same.

She looked around the room and took a deep breath. The floor was littered with old boards and odds and ends from the barn, and everything was covered in a thick layer of dust and dirt. It would take a huge effort to fix up this place.

"Uh-oh..." Marybeth turned to Jessica with a big smile. "Hey, it's a big job, but we can do it! I don't think we're going to finish before lunchtime, though."

Jessica picked up her mop bucket and broom and tried to gather some of Marybeth's optimism. But at the moment, she doubted they'd be done by the time their first guests arrived.

NINE

Jessica put down her broom and inspected her work. All of the extra boxes had been moved into another outbuilding and the loose lumber lay stacked in a neat pile outside the door. She and her mom and Marybeth had spent the last four hours sweeping, cleaning, and dusting the back half of the bunkhouse. As soon as they had the entire thing sufficiently cleaned, her father and brother would take over and put in the walls and closets. How would they ever get this place livable in three weeks?

Some of the neighbors had volunteered to help with the building of the barn. Maybe they could enlist a few of them to help with the bunkhouses, too.

She heard the growl of the tractor outside. Her father was preparing a spot for the new barn to be built. Dozens of large poles had been delivered earlier this morning. By tomorrow, they would be put in the ground and the barn would start to take shape.

It felt strange to think of a new stable going up when the acrid odor of the old burned barn still lingered. She thought about Rusty and how lucky it was that Duncan had rescued him from the fire. It was a very brave thing to do—and sad, too, since his own horse had to be put down. She felt thankful that her brother hadn't been hurt. Just the thought of it made her shiver.

She picked up a rag and wiped off a dust spot they had missed. From the old, narrow window she could see the training pen where her brother was working with the new horses. Their dog, Shep, ran around the outside of the pen, hoping for a chance to go in and help herd the horses.

Duncan has the best job, Jessica thought. He got to spend the entire morning out with the horses, getting them used to being handled again. She would much rather be outside with her brother than inside doing housework. But then she reminded herself about all the kids her own age who would be here in just a few weeks' time. Having new friends to hang out with would make it all worthwhile.

"Okay, ladies. I think it's time to see about lunch." Mrs. Warner pulled the plastic gloves from her hands and laid them over the side of the mop bucket. "Anyone interested in grilled hamburgers and hotdogs?"

"Yes!" Jessica and Marybeth said in unison.

Mrs. Warner wiped the dirt smudges from her face. "Jess, could you go tell your dad and Duncan that lunch will be ready in about twenty minutes? Marybeth, how about if you help me with the grilling?"

"Sure!" Marybeth pulled off her gloves and followed Mrs. Warner out the door.

Jessica went to the sink in the cabin's bathroom and

washed her face and hands. The grime on her cheeks felt at least an inch thick. Yuck! But the cold water felt good on her warm skin. The temperatures were getting hotter as summer approached, and the forecast for today was eighty-seven degrees. The heat in the bunkhouses would be stifling by the afternoon. They'd need to get air conditioning, or at least some big fans, before the dudes arrived.

She turned off the faucet and headed outside to where her father was moving lumber into position for the barn. She waved, trying to get his attention above the loud noise of the tractor. "Lunch, twenty minutes!" she hollered when he finally looked her way. Her father nodded and kept working.

Jessica turned and made her way to Rusty's corral to check on the two horses. It was time to put ointment on the poor gelding's wounds. When she reached the pen, she was delighted to see Chase walking with no limp. Her father's old remedy had worked miracles. Maybe by tomorrow she'd be able to practice a few of Duncan's training methods on the filly.

She got out the medicine and Rusty walked over to say hello. He laid his whiskered muzzle alongside her cheek and blew warm horse breath on her face. "I love you, too," she said, placing a kiss on the end of his nose. Rusty lifted his lip in a horse laugh and she knew she had tickled him. "Sorry about that, pal. Now just stand there like a good boy while I doctor these wounds."

Jessica was pleased that Rusty's burns were healing nicely. She was also glad to see that the filly was standing much closer to her now and didn't seem very alarmed about it. That gave her hope. She left the corral with an extra spring in her step.

When she reached the round pen where her brother was working the new horses, Jessica saw the blue roan haltered and walking calmly behind Duncan. She thought about the wild-eyed colt that she and Marybeth had watched racing around the pen just yesterday. Her brother had predicted the colt would be halter broke by the end of today. It seemed he'd been right.

"Mom says lunch'll be ready soon." Jessica watched the horse follow Duncan around the pen. When her brother stopped, the colt stopped. When he turned, the roan turned. What had happened between last night and now to make the colt seem docile as a puppy dog? "Can you show me some more training stuff?" she asked.

Duncan lifted his head enough to see out from underneath his ball cap. "Later," he said, then turned toward the gate and led the colt from the training circle.

Later? For Dunce, that could mean ten minutes from now, or next year. She watched him lead the gelding back to his pen, hoping that he'd invite her along and give her some more tips, but he just kept walking. At this rate, she'd *never* learn to train horses.

* * * * *

The next few days passed in a blur of cobwebs and cleaning rags, but at last they had one cabin cleaned and more-or-less remodeled, ready for visitors.

Jessica stood in the middle of the largest bunkhouse. This might be the building that would house her future best friends. A twang of guilt poked at her, reminding her of Marybeth and all the hours her sort-of best friend had spent on her knees scrubbing the floor when she didn't have to. According to Jessica's mother, that's what best friends did: helped each other with the tough stuff as well as being there for the fun things. She just wished Marybeth were a few years older. Sometimes she seemed grown up, but other times she acted like a baby.

"Let's call it a day," Mrs. Warner said, tossing her worn-out rag into the wastebasket. "Your father's gone up to the house, but I think Duncan wants to see you down at the corrals, Jess."

Marybeth checked her watch. "I'll see you tomorrow, Jess," she said. "My mom's supposed to be here soon to pick me up."

Jessica pulled off her gloves and laid them on a windowsill then waved goodbye to Marybeth. Her stomach rumbled, begging for dinner, but it could wait. Duncan had asked for her, and besides she wanted to check on Chase and Rusty.

Every day for the past three days, she'd gone to visit Rusty and Chase on her breaks from cabin cleaning. She'd taken carrots and apples, but nothing seemed to convince Storm Chaser to be friendly. Jessica could never get closer than six feet before the filly turned and walked away.

This baffled her. She could tell that the paint *wanted* to be friends. Chase stood there with ears pricked forward, looking very interested as Jessica brushed and pampered Rusty and fed him handfuls of goodies. But every time she approached, the filly hightailed it to the opposite end of the pen. Jessica remembered how her brother had tamed the roan colt to the halter in just one day. She wanted that so badly for Chase, too.

Unfortunately, Duncan had been too busy lately for Jessica to ask for his advice. He got up at daybreak to work on the barn, then spent the rest of his time breaking horses. There didn't seem to be any time left for her. Sometimes the Lightfoot boys dropped by to help and Jessica stood by the training pen, hoping that they'd invite her in. But they were too busy concentrating on the horses or laughing and joking around with each other to notice her. Not even Wyatt had turned to smile at her lately.

Who could figure boys out?

Jessica felt a rising surge of jealousy when she thought about Duncan having a good time with his best buddies. Her brother was so lucky to have kids his own age to do things with. Why did all the closest ranches have stupid boys living on them? They weren't any fun—well, maybe Wyatt, sort of—but the rest of them were a pain.

At least there was a good chance there would be girl visitors to the ranch. That idea brought a smile to Jessica's face and she quickened her step, but when she reached the corrals, she halted in her tracks.

Duncan stood in the middle of Rusty's pen while Wyatt waited outside the gate. Rusty wore a saddle and Chase had a lasso around her neck with the end of it snubbed to Rusty's saddle horn.

"What are you doing?" Jessica cried in alarm. "Rusty can't be ridden and Storm Chaser will choke if that lasso tightens."

"Stay where you are and be quiet!" Duncan ordered. His voice was low and urgent, and his blue eyes flashed.

Wyatt nodded and held up a hand to motion her to stay in place.

Jessica crossed her arms, angry at Duncan and Wyatt for being so bossy. But how could she keep quiet? Her brother knew Rusty was *not* supposed to be ridden. But as she watched him speak softly to the animals, her doubts began to fade.

Duncan quieted Chase with the low, steady drone of his voice. When the paint stood calmly, her ears forward, he picked up Rusty's lead rope and led him forward. Wyatt opened the gate for him. Chase balked when the rope tightened and Jessica feared there would be an accident. But the filly soon stepped forward, falling into line behind Rusty as he exited the pen. Both horses followed Duncan to the round pen. Wyatt walked quietly beside them.

When they were inside the training circle, Duncan quickly untied the rope from the saddle horn and handed Rusty to Wyatt. The Paiute boy tied the gelding to a tree. Jessica looked to her brother. "What are you going to do with Chase? How are you going to get the rope off her when we can't even touch her?"

Duncan shrugged. "Who says I want to take the rope off?"

With that, he took a firm grip on the loose end of the rope and smooched Chase into a lope. The spirited filly cocked her tail over her back and ran in a wide circle around Duncan, snorting and tossing her head as her hooves churned the sand under her feet. Her injured foot seemed to be totally healed.

"Wow, look at her go!" Jessica said to Wyatt, who had come to stand beside her. Rusty whinnied in concern. "Don't worry, she's okay," Jessica told the old horse. "She's just blowing off steam and feeling good."

She watched the paint, marveling at her speed and agility. Storm Chaser's muscles rippled under her shiny coat as she cantered around the ring. Jessica imagined climbing aboard the beautiful horse's back, feeling the power of the paint's stride and the sting of mane whipping against her face as they raced across the Nevada desert.

But Chase isn't mine, Jessica thought, *and she never will be.* She'd lost the filly before she ever really had her.

Before the barn burned, there might have been a small possibility of owning Chase. But now that dream was out of the question.

"This filly is one beautiful animal," Wyatt said, shifting his hat down low over his eyes. "I worked with her a lot when she was young, and I didn't want my dad to sell her. She's smart like her mama. Once she comes around and remembers what she was taught a while back, she's going to be one heck of a horse."

Storm Chaser made another quick round of the pen and Duncan let her slow down to a trot. He nodded for Jessica to enter the pen. She waited for the paint to pass the gate, then quickly squeezed through the bars and ran to the center of the round pen to stand beside her brother.

The black-and-white filly circled at a trot, still bucking and kicking up sand. "What do you want me to do?" Jessica asked.

Duncan handed her the end of the rope. "Okay, Jess, I want you to get a halter on this filly before we go up to the house for lunch."

Great, Jessica thought. *Now I'll have my first huge failure. And in front of Wyatt, too.* Chase hadn't let her within four feet of her head since she'd arrived at the ranch. How could she get a halter on her? She was going to flunk out of Duncan's training program—with Wyatt watching.

TEN

Jessica gulped. She had a hard time just trying to make a horse turn on cue. How could Duncan expect her to halter Storm Chaser in only twenty minutes? She kept her eyes on Chase as the paint circled the round pen with her tail in the air.

"What now?" she asked her brother.

Duncan leaned on the outside of the pen. "Let her canter a few more rounds in that direction and then make her turn and go the other way. But watch out. When she turns, it's going to put that rope around her hindquarters, and maybe up under her tail. When that happens, most horses go a little crazy. She'll probably start bucking and hopping around pretty good until she figures out that it's nothing that's going to hurt her. But that's what we want. She needs to figure it out on her own."

"But what if I can't hold onto her?" Jessica said, beginning to panic as her mind raced every which way. What if she got hurt—just like her father feared?

"You'll do fine," Wyatt said confidently. "You're in a round pen. She can't go anywhere but in circles." He grinned at her, and she heard Wyatt chuckle.

Sure, Jessica thought. It was easy for her brother and Wyatt to make jokes. They'd done this a hundred times. Keeping her eyes on the filly, she slowly reached down and picked up the lunge whip Duncan had left in the middle of the pen.

She took a deep breath and stepped one foot forward, hoping she was ahead of the imaginary line that would cause the filly to turn. Chase slammed on the brakes, setting her heels and hindquarters low and spinning in the opposite direction. She ran several steps and Jessica began to release the breath she'd been holding.

That's when all chaos broke loose. Just as Duncan had predicted, the rope ran up under Chase's tail, and the rodeo was on! Chase shot forward and Jessica cried out as the rope bit into her hands.

"Stay with her, Jess!" Duncan shouted from where he stood on the rail. "Make her go faster so she lines out and stops that bucking. Get her to do what you ask. Show her you're the one in charge. Horses respect and follow the lead horse. You've got to prove to her that the lead horse is *you.*"

Jessica lifted the lunge whip and cracked it in the air. There was no need to touch the horse with it. Chase would run from the sound. "Get up," she commanded, in as steady a voice as she could manage. She held onto the rope, giving and taking with the motion of the horse as Chase continued to buck, trying to rid herself of the rope under her tail.

After another round, the rope swung free, the bucking slowed, and the filly continued around the ring at a steady rhythm. Jessica allowed herself a small smile. *I can do this!* she told herself.

"Good job, Jess," Wyatt praised her.

"Now tell your horse what a good girl she is, too," Duncan said. "Let her hear the sound of your voice, and keep it light and pleasant. She's doing what you want. Reward her with your voice and let her break into a trot. See the way her inside ear is tipping toward you? She's paying attention now."

Jessica nodded. The filly did seem to be paying attention to her. "Good girl, Chase," she crooned, and was delighted to see the paint's full blaze swing in her direction as she continued to trot the circle. "That's my good girl."

"Excellent!" Duncan said. "Make her go another two rounds. Then make your body go quiet and ask her to whoa. We want Chase to halt and turn in to face you."

The next two rounds felt like an eternity as Jessica gripped the end of the rope, waiting to see if Chase would give her the desired response. When the time came, she laid down the whip, let her free arm hang at her sides, and said, "Whoa, girl, whoa." The paint trotted another half-length of the pen, her ears flicking to the center to gauge what Jessica was asking.

The paint pulled herself to a walk, then halted and turned into the center, taking two extra steps toward Jessica.

Jessica held out her hand, beckoning the filly to come to her. But Chase stayed in place, her coat sweaty and her sides heaving from the run. The paint's nostrils extended, blowing and sniffing, trying to catch Jess's scent.

Duncan climbed through the rails and entered the pen.

"Nice work, Jess. I'll take over now and get that rope off her neck."

Chase shifted her feet but stood where she was, watching the two of them.

"I thought I was supposed to put a halter on her," Jessica said.

Wyatt and Duncan laughed. "I was just kidding," her brother said. "You go on up to the house. I'll get the halter on her and be right up."

"Yeah, right." Jessica chuckled. There was no way her brother would get that halter on Chase in the next five minutes. She wished she could watch him try, but she heard her mother calling them to their nightly meal. She waved to the boys and headed to the house.

She let herself in through the back door and washed her hands in the kitchen sink, wondering if Wyatt would be joining them for dinner. Ten minutes later, Duncan walked into the kitchen by himself, and Jessica felt both disappointed and relieved. She was starving, but she wasn't sure she could manage to eat with him across the table.

Duncan had a huge grin on his face as he stuck his hands under the faucet.

"What are you so happy about, Dunce?" Jessica asked, following her brother to the table.

Duncan shrugged and filled his plate with spaghetti. Once he started shoveling it into his mouth, Jess knew he wouldn't answer her question. But she had a sneaking suspicion it had to do with Chase.

Mrs. Warner passed the salad and Jessica put some on her

plate, being careful not to get any of the onions or green peppers.

"Just another few days of hard work and the cabins will be ready," Mrs. Warner said.

"I'll be down to check on the plumbing tomorrow morning," Mr. Warner said, stuffing a big bite of garlic bread into his mouth. "The lumberyard will be delivering another load of boards in the afternoon. That'll keep Dunce and me busy for a while. The Lightfoots are coming over tomorrow to help with the framing."

Jessica dug into her meal with gusto. In a little over a week, their guests would be here!

They'd already been discussing various ranch activities for the visitors: swimming in the lake, hiking, fishing in one of the nearby streams, riding the trails, playing horseshoes. They'd even planned a cattle drive. Everyone would take turns introducing the guests to the different trails and activities. Some things the guests could do on their own, once they were familiar with the routine. The big events like the weenie roast, the hayride, and the cattle drive would be handled by her parents.

Just wait until I tell Marybeth about the cattle drive, Jessica thought. She should ask her parents if her friend could go. After all the hard work the kid had put in, she doubted her mom and dad would say no. Marybeth would love it…especially if there were other girls there her age. Maybe if she had friends her own age, she wouldn't be so interested in hanging around with Jessica.

Jessica had never been on a cattle drive, even though her

family moved the herd every year. She'd always stayed home with her mom while her father, Duncan, and the Lightfoot boys made the trip. But this year, everyone was going. The only problem was she didn't have a horse of her own to put a saddle on. She couldn't ride Rusty, and she sure didn't want to ride Grizz.

You had to stay on your toes if you rode that ornery nag. It wasn't that he liked to buck or rear, but if you didn't pay close attention, he'd turn around and bite your leg while you were in the saddle. Or untie himself from the hitching line and run home without you. And he wasn't above making a fast turn to see if you'd tumble out of the saddle.

She didn't understand why her dad was worried about her working with the new horses, but didn't seem to be bothered by her riding Grizz. Grizzly always minded her father—but he knew how stubborn that horse could be with other riders. She'd much rather take her chances with Storm Chaser.

Jessica missed riding Rusty. He was totally trustworthy and they'd had some great times together. But even though the old horse was coughing less and his burns were healing, he still wasn't in any condition to bear a rider. He seemed to enjoy his retirement and the companionship of Storm Chaser. She couldn't begrudge him that after all the faithful years he'd carried her.

When dinner ended, Jessica helped her mother wash the dishes, then went down to the horse pens to say good night to Chase and Rusty. She was shocked to see Duncan leading the paint around the training pen—in her blue halter!

For an instant, she felt a twinge of jealousy, wishing she'd been the one who'd put the halter on Chase for the first time. But she quickly dismissed that thought. Once Chase was halter broke, there were all kinds of things Jessica could do with her. "How did you do that?" she asked.

Duncan just smiled and handed her the filly's lead rope. "Walk her around the pen a few times so she gets used to you. Try to touch her all over. She's pretty good for a horse that just came off the range. I'll work with her a little more on haltering, and then she's all yours. Holler if you need help getting her back into her pen. I think she'll be fine."

Jessica watched as her brother walked away. Now that he acted like he trusted her to handle Storm Chaser, she felt as if she didn't really know anything.

Duncan turned to face her as he backed away. "Come on, Jess, you've been watching Dad and me train horses your entire life. You know what to do."

Her brother was right, Jessica realized. She knew the basics. And she was sure he would help if she got stuck. She just needed some practice and a little more confidence.

She stared dreamily into Chase's soft brown eyes, imagining herself climbing into the saddle for the first ride. Her father certainly wouldn't allow that. He was afraid she'd get hurt. But he hadn't said anything about ground work.

Jessica pursed her lips and tried to ignore her uncertainty. Maybe her father's ban on horse training did include ground work, but he hadn't specifically mentioned it. If she stayed off Chase's back, she was fairly sure she could stay out of trouble with her dad.

It would probably be Duncan, Wyatt, or Gator who would

be the first to ride Storm Chaser. Another flare of jealousy bloomed inside Jessica, but again she tamped it down. Her brother and his friends would be good to Chase and they'd do it right. It was the best she could hope for.

Chase walked calmly beside Jessica, and the two of them circled the ring several times. Jessica slowed and gave a slight downward tug on the lead rope, asking the filly to stand still. Chase halted, but stepped to the side, eyeing her with unease. "It's okay," Jess said, offering her hand, palm up, to the filly.

Chase extended her nose, and Jessica felt the tickle of the paint's whiskers on her fingers. "That's my girl," she said softly, then carefully placed her hand on the filly's jaw, rubbing in a slow circle. Chase stiffened at first, then relaxed under the touch. She actually seemed to enjoy it.

Jessica smiled and moved her hand to the paint's neck, working her way to the horse's shoulder and midsection. She tried to keep her actions slow and steady and her voice low and gentle so as not to startle the filly and cause her to lose trust. When she worked her way down one side and the filly seemed at ease, she went to the offside and started again.

This side wasn't as easy, but Jessica took her time, just the way she'd seen her father and brother do. After a few extra minutes, Chase relaxed and allowed Jessica to move around her quietly without flinching.

"Thank you," Jessica whispered and smiled as Storm Chaser's ears pricked forward, trying to catch the sound of her voice. "You are wonderful!"

Jessica made one more trip around the pen and then

walked the filly toward the gate. Did she dare return Chase to Rusty's corral by herself? What if something startled the young horse and she pulled back and got loose? She put her hand on Chase's neck. "Can I trust you to behave yourself if I promise not to make any fast moves?"

Chase just stared blankly at her.

"Okay, here we go," Jessica said feeling a lump of apprehension rise up in her throat. She opened the gate slowly and sighed with relief when the young paint didn't shy away but followed her through and continued in the direction of Rusty's corral.

Jessica smiled. "You know exactly where we're going, don't you, girl?" She laid her hand softly on Chase's neck again. "And I bet you know there's food waiting for you when we get there, huh? I'll be sure you get an extra snack tonight for being so good."

When Jessica and Chase reached the pen, Rusty belted out a greeting, his sides shaking with the force of his whinny. Jessica walked through the gate, shut it, and gently removed the halter from Chase's head. The filly immediately took her place beside Rusty at the feeder.

Jessica stepped back in satisfaction. She had actually helped train a horse today. She couldn't wait until tomorrow to try it again!

ELEVEN

"You are so lucky," Marybeth said with a sigh as Jessica put on her helmet and placed her boot into the stirrup to climb up behind her. Daisy, the Appaloosa pony, flicked her tail in annoyance at the added weight, but did as she was asked and walked off at a brisk pace. "I wish I could learn how to train horses." Marybeth turned in the saddle. "Hey, do you think when I'm a little older, your brother will teach me, too?"

Jessica chuckled. "You never know with Dunce. I'm his sister and I'm never sure when he's going to work with me."

"What about Wyatt?" Marybeth said. "I bet he'd help if you asked him. And he's kinda cute."

Jessica shrugged. "I never thought about it." But her heart thumped a little harder at the mention of the Paiute boy's name.

Marybeth looked over her shoulder. "That's such a fib. You always get all embarrassed when he talks to you."

Jessica gave her friend a playful slug in the shoulder, then grabbed the back of the saddle as the startled pony broke into a canter. The girls both laughed and held on tight until Marybeth had Daisy back under control.

"What do you know about boys?" Jessica said.

Marybeth shrugged. "I may not know all that much about boys, but I know you get all freaked out whenever Wyatt's around."

"I do not." Jessica tweaked her friend's ponytail.

"Whatever," Marybeth said.

For the rest of the ride around the ranch, Jessica filled Marybeth in on the details of the activities her parents had planned for the vacationers.

"A cattle drive!" Marybeth exclaimed. "That would be so awesome! I've always wanted to go on one. I'll ask my parents as soon as I get home."

"I still need to ask my parents and make sure it's okay, but I'm sure they'll be cool with it. You worked as hard as we did," Jessica said. "You deserve to go."

Marybeth reined her pony around a clump of sage brush and headed back toward the house. "Just think, Jess, we're going to meet a whole bunch of kids with this guest ranch thing."

"I hope so," Jessica said. "We don't have any control over who signs up. But my mom said there were definitely girls in this first group."

"Good," Marybeth said. "It's about time we got some girls around here."

Marybeth dropped Jessica off at the front door, waved a quick goodbye, and trotted off toward home.

* * * * *

The next week passed in a flurry of activity as everyone continued to work hard to finish the preparations for the vacationers. Jessica worked with Storm Chaser some nights after dinner when the chores were done. She half-expected her mom or dad to see her and say something. She still harbored a suspicion that her father wouldn't be pleased to find out how much she was doing with Chase. But the part of her that really loved working with the filly overruled her sense of responsibility.

Chase was smart and picked things up quickly. Duncan showed Jessica how to "sack out" a new horse by taking a soft gunny sack and rubbing it over every inch of the horse's body, then flapping it around so the horse would get used to scary, floppy things.

Next came lunging, where Chase learned to walk, trot, and canter in a circle around Jessica at the end of a long lunge line. When the filly settled into that, Duncan stepped in and showed Jessica how to ground-drive a horse with a pair of long lead lines attached to the halter. Chase needed to be taught to steer, stop, and back up without carrying a rider.

"It makes things a whole lot easier when it's time to mount up," Duncan said. "There's nothing I hate worse than getting dropped in the dirt."

"Do you think it's time to put a saddle on Chase?" Jessica asked. "It's only been a week since we started working with her."

Duncan reached out to scratch Storm Chaser's neck. "She's really smart, Jess. She's picked everything up really quickly so far… a lot quicker than the colts I'm working with.

Wyatt kind of took a liking to this filly when she was young and worked with her a lot. I guess Chase remembers it and she's tamed right down."

"Does that mean we could start riding her soon?"

"Who's *we?*" Duncan asked. "You know Dad would ground us both for life if I let you up on this filly before she's safe. He probably won't be too happy with what I've already let you do."

Jessica sighed. "I know he'd be really mad, but it would be so cool to ride her. It might even be worth getting in trouble for."

Three days later, Jessica hadn't even put a foot in Chase's stirrup, but she got in trouble anyway.

"What do you mean 'she's only doing ground work'?" Mr. Warner's voice echoed across the stable yard as he confronted Duncan. "I thought I made it perfectly clear that your sister is too young to start training horses."

Duncan hung his head and scuffed at the dirt beneath his boots. "I'm sorry, Dad. I thought you were talking about *riding* the horses. I wasn't going to let Jess up on Storm Chaser until the filly was safe and you said okay."

"Well, it isn't *safe* for her to be doing ground work with that filly either," Mr. Warner went on. "You know how easy it is to get hurt when working with young stock."

Jessica stood in the round pen, resting the long lines in her hands as her brother and father argued.

"But she's doing really well," Duncan said, leading their father to the round pen. "Jess, show Dad what you've taught Chase."

Jessica's heart hammered in her chest when she saw the unhappy look on her father's face. She and Duncan were in major trouble. Her father hadn't specifically forbidden her from doing ground work with Chase, but she knew she'd cheated by going around his authority. Her hands shook on the long lines as she moved the filly in a circle around her. She ran her through her paces, asking for a walk, trot, and canter, as well as turns and stops.

Chase performed admirably. Jessica patted her and gave her a treat when they were finished.

Mr. Warner tipped his hat back and sighed. "I've got to admit, Jess, you've done a good job with this filly."

Jessica felt herself swell with pride. Her father had praised her for training Storm Chaser!

"Unfortunately, however, you both disobeyed my orders," Mr. Warner continued. "Maybe I could have been a little more specific, but I think you both knew what I was talking about."

He turned to Duncan. "Your punishment is going to be added chores, and no riding out with the Lightfoot boys for the next couple days."

Duncan frowned heavily. Jessica felt badly for her brother. She knew how much he enjoyed the wild rides across the desert with his friends. He'd only been trying to help her, and now he was in trouble for it.

Mr. Warner spoke to Jessica. "And you, young lady, will have extra chores, too. But right now, I would like you to take the tack off of that filly, brush her down, and return her to the pen with the rest of the new stock. She'll be under your brother's care and you are not to do anything with this horse until I say so."

He looked at both of them. "Am I perfectly understood?"

Duncan nodded.

"Yes, sir," Jessica said, feeling miserable. She patted Chase and walked her over to the hitching post to remove her equipment and brush her. Then she took her to Rusty's corral so Chase could say goodbye.

"I'm sorry, ol' boy," she said as she watched the horses touch noses. "I got us all into trouble, so now you're going to lose your stable buddy for a while."

Rusty nickered and nudged Chase with his muzzle. Jessica wanted to cry. She'd grown close to the paint filly over the past week. And spending time apart was going to hurt both her and Rusty. Maybe she'd be able to talk Duncan into bringing Chase over to visit the old horse when he'd finished working with her for the day. Just because she was being punished was no reason to punish Rusty.

Duncan stood at the stock pen gate and opened it for Jessica when she arrived. "I'm really sorry, Dunce," Jessica said. She unbuckled the halter from Chase's finely shaped head and watched the paint walk into the herd of geldings, swishing her tail and pinning her ears at the ones who got too close. "This wasn't your fault. I know you were just trying to help me, and now I've gotten you into trouble."

Duncan shrugged. "Hey, it's only for a while. I'll be so busy, it'll fly by." He smiled and walked off.

Jessica breathed a small sigh of relief. At least her brother wasn't upset with her. She turned and followed him up to the house. The guests would be arriving soon. She might as well get started on the million things they had left to do. Maybe it would take her mind off of not being able to see Chase.

* * * * *

Jessica unfolded the new bed sheet and shook it out, tossing one side of it to Marybeth. Her friend giggled when it landed on her head and she blindly walked into the bed, bumping her knee on the post.

Mrs. Warner laughed. "By the time you girls finish making all these beds, our guests will be here."

Still grinning, Jessica pulled the sheet from Marybeth's head and centered it on the twin-sized bed, tucking the excess under the mattress. "Just think of all the new friends we'll have to hang out with."

Mrs. Warner brought over an armful of blankets and put one on each of the eight beds in the bunkhouse. "I know you girls are getting excited about meeting the visitors, but just keep in mind that it isn't always easy to make friends right off the bat."

Jessica furrowed her brow. She hadn't thought about that.

"As owners of this ranch and the hosts for our guests," Mrs. Warner continued, "we need to be aware of their needs. Sometimes people want to socialize and sometimes they just want to be left alone." She smiled at Jessica. "As a representative of this ranch, you will be expected to abide by the guests' wishes in that department. Understood?"

"Yes, ma'am."

Mrs. Warner brushed a lock of Jessica's hair behind her ears. "I'm sure they'll be a friendly bunch," she reassured her. "I know how much you girls are looking forward to having some other gals your age to hang out with. I just want to make sure you understand that you should be friendly and accommodating to all the guests, but it will be up to them how much contact they want to have with us ranch hands."

She looked out the bunkhouse window. "Oh, my, Jess, I think there's something out there you might want to see," she said.

Jessica and Marybeth crowded to the window. A movement in the training pen caught Jessica's eye and her mouth dropped open.

Duncan sat astride Chase, and the filly trotted around the pen as if she'd been doing it forever. Storm Chaser was being trained to ride!

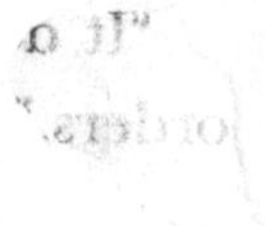

TWELVE

Jessica bolted for the door with Marybeth right on her heels. She stopped about a hundred yards from the round pen where Duncan worked Chase. She knew she wasn't allowed to be near the filly right now. No sense taking the risk of angering her father again.

She thrilled to the sight of the little paint trotting around the pen with her ears pricked, waiting for a cue from her rider. Her father stood outside the circle, giving Duncan pointers. After a moment, he looked up and motioned the two girls over.

They walked forward slowly, not wanting to spook the young horse.

"It's all right," Mr. Warner said, making room on the rail for her and Marybeth. "This filly is rock-solid. She's got a good mind and learns quickly." He clapped Jessica on the shoulder. "You did a real good job with her, Jess."

Jessica smiled at the praise.

[illegible]oesn't mean I've forgotten that you two skirted my [illegible]," he warned. "But you did a fine job with this filly. I think maybe you've got the Warner horse trainer's touch."

Jessica hoped her father was right. And maybe, just maybe, he would let her work with Chase again soon. "Watch this," Duncan said as he trotted the filly in a figure-eight pattern, then asked her to canter the full ring. "She's broke as well as any of the horses I've had in training for thirty days. And I've only been on her three times."

Mr. Warner nodded. "Well, this filly's momma is that nice black-and-white paint mare I've been trying to buy from the Lightfoots for the past three years. All of her colts are easygoing and smart. She's going to be just like her momma." He took off his hat and brushed a hand through his hair. "I sure wish we could afford to keep her. This filly would be a nice addition to the ranch."

Jessica's heart sank. She didn't need to be reminded that Chase would be sold to another ranch and she might not ever see her again. Marybeth grabbed her hand and squeezed it. Jessica gave the younger girl a smile, but she was sure it looked rather sickly.

Mr. Warner plopped his hat back on his head and motioned Duncan to pull the filly up to the fence. "I've been thinking…you and Jess have been working awfully hard these past few days without any complaints. Can I assume that you've both learned your lesson?" He looked from one to the other, waiting for their nods. "Okay then, you are both off of suspension."

Jessica breathed a deep sigh of relief. "Does this mean I can move Chase back in with Rusty? He misses her a lot."

Her father chuckled. "*Rusty* misses her, huh?"

Jessica nodded and her father laughed harder.

"I'm pretty sure it isn't just Rusty who misses her," he said as he reached out and ruffled his daughter's hair.

Jessica returned his grin. "Okay, maybe I miss her a little bit, too."

"Well, like I said before," her father cautioned. "Don't get too attached to this filly. She'll bring a good price." He smiled down at Jessica and softened his words. "Honey, I know you had your eye on this little paint to replace Rusty, and I wish I could do it. But we're strapped for cash, and we need to sell every single one of these new horses."

Jessica looked down at the ground. The ranch had to come before her wishes. She knew that. But her heart ached just the same.

She waited until Duncan finished with the paint, then led Storm Chaser back to Rusty's pen. The old gelding nickered a warm greeting and met them at the gate. "Go on, get back," Jessica said, shooing him away from the entrance so she could get Chase through the gate.

"Your buddy is back," she said to Rusty. "But try not to get too attached to her this time. Dad says we've got to sell her, and Duncan's doing pretty well with her, so we probably won't get to keep her much longer."

Just saying the words was almost impossible. Everyone had warned her not to fall in love with the awesome black-and-white filly, but it was too late. *Much too late.*

* * * * *

"Here they come!" Marybeth galloped Daisy up the road at top speed. "They just pulled onto the lower road."

The Warners and Marybeth stood in the front yard, watching as two dual-cab trucks pulling horse trailers turned onto the dirt road leading to Wild Hawk Ranch.

Jessica thought the trucks and trailers looked pretty fancy. She glanced around the ranch, wondering if the visitors would think it looked okay. Their house was old and probably needed a new coat of paint. There was nothing special about their yard, and the new barn was just a series of poles sticking out of the ground, with two-by-fours creating the frame. It still needed siding and a roof.

But the bunkhouses were fixed up pretty nicely. She and Marybeth had placed fresh flowers in pitchers and vases beside each bed. And they'd planned some fun activities and great horseback rides for the vacationers. They were sure the kids would really like the weenie roasts, barbeques, and trips to the lake.

They waited while the vehicles made slow progress up the bumpy road. Jessica grinned as she watched Duncan shift nervously from foot to foot. He didn't like meeting new people. He glanced toward the horse pens, and she knew her brother was probably wishing he were out there with the horses instead of standing here waiting to greet guests.

The trucks rolled into the driveway and her father guided them back to the stable area where there was room to turn around. Jessica and Marybeth followed along behind the horse trailers. The trucks came to a stop and people started piling out. Jessica was thrilled to see two girls and a boy pop out of the first truck. The boy appeared to be about fourteen or fifteen. He waved to her brother and said "hi." Duncan just nodded in the boy's direction.

The girls appeared to be a year or two older than Jessica. She guessed that they were probably friends, and not sisters. The taller one had black hair and was very thin, while the shorter girl was plump with red hair.

The door to the other truck opened, and after the parents stepped out, a boy her age jumped from the cab and stretched his long legs. "Hi, I'm Michael," he said to everyone with a friendly smile, then pointed over his shoulder toward the truck. "And that slowpoke inside is my sister, Ariel. Get out here, Ari. It's time to start our vacation!"

A tall, willowy girl with long blonde hair exited gracefully from the truck. She wore a snug pair of fancy jeans, an expensive pair of leather boots, and a shirt that would have made a rodeo queen green with envy. Jessica thought she was probably one of the prettiest girls she had ever seen. Ariel looked around the ranch, then wrinkled her nose and frowned. "What is that weird musty smell? And where are we going to put Raven? There's no barn here. The brochure showed a picture of a barn."

Jessica frowned. *Musty smell?*

Marybeth elbowed her in the ribs. "She must be talking about the sagebrush," she whispered.

Jessica huffed. Sagebrush smelled wonderful!

A loud clank of hoof on metal sounded as the horse inside

Ariel and Michael's trailer kicked the wall and whinnied. Several of the ranch horses, including Rusty and Chase, answered the distressed cry.

"That must be Raven," Jessica whispered back.

They watched as Ariel and Michael's father opened the trailer doors. Ariel ran inside, clucking like a worried hen. Jessica could hear the girl shouting orders to her father from inside the trailer.

She looked to her own parents to see how they were responding. Her mother had a worried expression on her face, and her father definitely looked disturbed. No way would Jessica get away with talking to her parents like that. She'd be grounded for life!

A moment later, hoofbeats sounded on the trailer floor and Ariel and Raven stepped out.

"Wow," Marybeth said, her jaw dropping in awe.

Jessica let out a low whistle. "*Amazing.*" Raven stood at least seventeen hands—his back was eight inches taller than her head. And his solid black coat shone like the back of a crow's wing. He had a white star in the middle of his forehead and one hind white foot. Raven appeared to be some kind of a fancy Warmblood show horse.

The large black horse lifted his head, which made him seem even taller, and eyed the large tract of open desert. Jessica could see the muscles quiver under his slick coat as his nostrils widened to take in the different scents. A moment later, he lifted his tail over his back, snorted, and jerked on the lead rope, pulling Ariel along beside him like a skier on a lake.

Duncan ran forward, removing his hat from his head. He held it in the air in front of the horse to get the big guy's attention. Raven stopped for a second. Duncan grabbed the rope from Ariel, turned the horse to the side, and gave an attention-getting jerk on the halter.

The excitable horse lowered his head and stood still.

Ariel, surprised at having her horse taken from her, looked as if she were about to scream at Duncan. But she stopped short when he gave her an amused look and handed back Raven's lead rope.

The girl's face turned from anger to a huge smile in an instant. She brushed her long blonde hair out of her eyes and gave Jessica's brother a dazzling smile as she accepted the rope. Duncan smiled back, then turned on his heels and walked away, leaving everyone else to help settle in the horses and new visitors for their stay.

"Ariel, maybe you should let your father take Raven to his stall," Mrs. Wilson said. "He seems to have a lot of energy today."

"That's okay." Ariel kept hold of the lead rope. "I can handle him. Why don't you and Dad get all of Raven's things and bring them down to his stall?"

"Jess," Mrs. Warner said. "Could you please show the Wilsons where to put Raven? I'll help the Curtis family settle their horses in, then everyone can join us in the main bunkhouse for introductions and orientation. We'll give the guests a quick rundown on what they can expect for this week."

Jessica wished she could have helped the Curtis family.

Melissa and her brother seemed really nice. Ariel was so regal that Jessica was almost afraid to talk to her.

The blast of a truck horn sounded in the driveway, and everyone turned to see the last family of vacationers enter the stable yard. They were from California and they weren't pulling a trailer. Apparently they would be riding ranch horses.

"Everyone, these are the Turners," Mr. Warner announced when they stepped out of their vehicle.

Mr. Turner smiled and nodded. "My name is Dean, and this is my wife, Betty, and our kids, Mark and Lainey."

Jessica heard Ariel snort. "*Lainey?*" she said in a snide voice to the other kids standing around her. They giggled.

Jessica felt bad for Lainey, who didn't even seem to notice that anyone was laughing at her name. It wasn't such a bad name—and it had been a mean thing for Ariel to say. Maybe she just felt tired and grouchy from the trip.

"Come on, Ariel," Marybeth piped up in her high-pitched voice. "We'll show you where you can put Raven. It's a nice portable stall with a roof where he can keep out of the sun."

Ariel gave Marybeth an odd look. "You aren't in charge, are you? And what do you mean, a portable stall? I thought this place was a *ranch.*"

Jessica walked beside Marybeth, leading the way to the stall. "We had a really bad fire a few weeks ago, and it burned down our barn."

"That's why they're operating as a dude ranch now," Marybeth volunteered. "Jessica's dad didn't want to, but they need to rebuild their barn and—"

"Here we are," Jessica interrupted her friend before she could spill any more family secrets. She frowned at Marybeth, who immediately cowered like a scolded puppy dog. She felt bad about that, but Marybeth didn't need to be telling everything she knew. Jessica opened the gate for Ariel to enter the portable stall and corral.

Ariel stared at the portable pen, but stayed outside. "Raven is used to staying in a box stall. He won't like this."

Jessica pursed her lips. She wanted new friends, but this particular girl was making things difficult. The portable stall was brand new, loaned to them by a rancher down the road. "It's all we have," Jessica said.

Ariel rolled her eyes and Jessica wished she'd been given charge of the other girls. They had to be friendlier than this one.

Duncan walked up with a wheelbarrow load of hay nets to hang for the horses' dinners.

Ariel perked up. "That's really nice of you to deliver Raven's dinner. I was just putting him in his pen." She walked her horse through the gate of the portable and took off his halter.

Jessica and Marybeth stared at each other, amazed at the transformation Ariel went through when Duncan came around. Jessica watched her brother shuffle into the pen with the hay net slung over his shoulder. Duncan was very shy around girls—especially pretty ones. He didn't say a word as he hung the hay net, but he gave the new girl a nice smile. Jessica felt like kicking him.

Ariel stared at Duncan expectantly, the smile still on her face.

"See ya," her brother muttered and quickly exited the pen.

"Thanks again, Duncan." Ariel continued to smile at his retreating back. "Maybe we can go for a ride later?"

"I'd like to go for a ride," Marybeth said.

Ariel blinked and turned to stare at Marybeth. "You're kind of young for me to hang around with," she said. "I used to babysit kids your age." She gave a quick nod to Jessica and sauntered off in the direction of the bunkhouses.

"Whoa..." Marybeth said under her breath.

"*Whoa* is right." Jessica shoved her hands deep into her pockets. Ariel was pretty and she had a great horse, but she didn't seem very nice. She sure did seem to like Duncan, though.

This might be a very *long* ten days.

THIRTEEN

The first evening at Wild Hawk Ranch, the guests mostly unpacked and settled in. Jessica's mother had spent the past several hours preparing the meal. Over a dinner of barbequed chicken, mashed potatoes, and corn on the cob, Jessica listened to her parents explain the activities that would be offered while they were there. Everyone seemed excited about the cattle drive and agreed it would be the highlight of the week. Jessica's parents had given the okay to let Marybeth come, and both girls were eagerly looking forward to the adventure.

"Raven has never seen a cow," Ariel said as she picked at her food and stared across the table at Duncan. "Maybe someone can ride with me until I know he won't act up."

"I'll ride with you," Marybeth volunteered. "Daisy isn't afraid of cows. It will be our first cattle drive, too. It would be fun to do it together."

Ariel frowned at the young girl and looked straight at Duncan. "Thanks for the offer, but I'd rather be near someone who's done this before and knows what he's doing."

Duncan helped himself to another piece of chicken. "Actually, it might be better if you did ride with Marybeth and Jess. I'll be busy making sure the cattle are quiet and heading in the right direction. The last thing we need is a stampede with a bunch of greenhorns out there."

"What's a greenhorn?" Marybeth asked.

Jessica helped herself to another ear of corn. "That would be us. We're green as grass and don't know anything about moving cattle."

"None of us has ever been on a cattle drive," Lainey chimed in, "so we'll all be pretty unsure of ourselves, Ariel. I think we should just stay together in the back and let the pros move those cows."

Sheri and Monica, the two friends who hadn't said much yet, nodded. "Cows scare me," Monica said. "They stink and they blow snot on everything."

"Yeah," Sheri agreed. "What if one decides to charge? Or what if my horse spooks?"

Mark chuckled. "That's why I'm riding one of the ATVs we brought with us. You girls can have your horses. I'm riding a steel horse."

The parents were all at the other end of the large table, but Jessica's dad must have heard them talking. He chuckled. "It won't be too difficult for you greenhorns," he said. "These cows have made the trip several times. They know where they're going and could probably get there without us. But we've got a lot of seasoned cowpokes riding on this drive. The Lightfoot boys will be helping out. They'll each be stationed at a specific point in the herd to make sure things go smoothly. If you want to learn something about driving cattle, I suggest you pair up with one of our cowboys. They'll keep you safe and show you the ropes."

Jessica perked up at the mention of the Lightfoots. Wyatt would be riding on the drive! She watched Ariel's eyes swing immediately to Duncan again at her father's suggestion of pairing up with a cowhand. But her brother kept his head down and continued shoveling food into his mouth. Jessica wasn't sure what was so attractive about Dunce, but everywhere he went, the girls fawned all over him.

Sheri, the girl with the short red hair, pushed aside her empty plate and spoke to Jessica. "Monica and I thought it would be really cool if you could show us some of the trails tomorrow."

Ariel looked at the girl and frowned. "I've already got tomorrow planned out," she said. "We should all go to the lake in the morning. It's supposed to be hot. Who wants to go with me?" She looked pointedly at Duncan, who kept his eyes on his plate.

Sheri and Monica exchanged looks and then shrugged. "Sure, that sounds good," Monica said. "We can catch some rays and do the trails later."

"Okay with me," Mark said. He turned to Ariel's brother, Michael. "Want to ride the other ATV?" he asked. "I'll ask my dad to see if it's okay."

"Sure," Michael said. "That'd be really cool. Ariel and my parents are the horse fans. I'd rather ride something with an engine in it." Everyone laughed.

"I'd like to go to the lake," Marybeth said with a wave of her hand.

Ariel raised an eyebrow. "Don't you want to stick around

here and play horseshoes with the grown-ups? Or maybe Jessica could do something with you?"

Jessica saw Marybeth's face fall. Why was Ariel being so mean to her? And why did Ariel think *she* should stay behind? Did that mean the girl thought *she* was a little kid, too?

"Marybeth has gone to that lake with me at least a hundred times," she said, defending her friend. "She'll be fine."

Jessica caught a warning look from her mother and remembered the speech she'd been given about not bothering the guests if they wanted to be left alone. But she really wanted to go to the lake, especially since all the other kids were going, too.

"Just making a suggestion," Ariel said with a shrug.

Duncan didn't say anything. But Ariel's brother did.

"Come on, Ari, lighten up," Michael said. "Jessica and Marybeth can go with us. Hey, it's their lake."

Jessica gave Michael a grateful smile.

"Too bad we can't drive to town," Ariel said. "I'll have my driver's license soon." She looked to see if Duncan was impressed.

Jessica finished her meal and folded her napkin. Most of their guests seemed pretty nice, but Ariel was proving to be a real pain.

* * * * *

The next morning, Jessica got up early and went down to the kitchen to help her mother prepare ham, toast, orange juice, and mounds of scrambled eggs while Duncan and her father went to feed the livestock. Breakfast was a noisy affair held at the long tables in the biggest bunkhouse, with everyone trying to talk at once. The adults chatted about riding out on the desert, while the kids planned their trip to the lake. Jessica volunteered to pack sandwiches for everyone, and Sheri and Lainey offered their help.

When breakfast was finished, the three girls trooped to the house and Jessica got out jars of peanut butter and jelly. They set up an assembly line and made enough sandwiches for everyone.

"This is going to be so exciting. I've never been on a vacation like this." Sheri spread a thick layer of peanut butter on the bread and passed it down to Lainey, who slapped on the grape jelly. Jessica put the two pieces of bread together and stuffed the sandwiches into a baggie.

"I think the cattle drive is going to be so awesome!" Lainey said, trying to wipe the hair out of her eyes and managing to leave a line of sticky goo across her cheek.

"How come you've never been on a cattle drive, Jessica?" Sheri asked. "I mean, you live here. And your dad told us they do this drive every year."

"My dad didn't think I was old enough to go." Jessica shrugged. "He's a little overprotective sometimes. But at least I'll get to go this year. It gets pretty lonely out here. Marybeth is the only girl close to my age for miles. It'll be nice to have all of you along."

"Except maybe Ariel," Sheri said.

Jessica wanted to agree, but she didn't dare. She had a

feeling her mother wouldn't approve of her talking about a guest behind her back. So she just smiled and stuffed the last sandwich into a baggie.

Sheri and Lainey went with the rest of the group to ready their horses while Jessica headed to the shed and retrieved the saddlebags. She brought them back to the kitchen and packed the sandwiches and enough drinks and apples for everyone.

As she returned from the new tack shed, a prebuilt tool shed they'd purchased with some of the insurance money, Jessica noticed Ariel and Michael standing outside the training pen watching Duncan as he worked the colts. Michael was asking Duncan a lot of questions. Jessica could see the strained look on her brother's face. But he seemed to be doing his best to answer the questions politely.

"We'll be leaving for the lake pretty soon," Jessica called to Ariel and Michael. "You'd better get your horse and ATV ready to go. Everyone else is saddling up now."

Marybeth rode down the driveway on Daisy. She had on a big straw hat and a T-shirt and shorts. The straps of her bathing suit peeked out from under her shirt, and a beach towel lay across the front of her saddle.

"Great," Ariel grouched. "Looks like the munchkin is definitely coming."

"Don't worry," Jessica said to Ariel as she hefted the saddlebags over her shoulder. "There's a lot of room at the lake. Marybeth and I won't be under your feet."

"Jess!" Mr. Warner hollered from the corrals when she led Grizz out to join Marybeth and Daisy. "Can I see you for a minute? Put your horse back in the pen and unsaddle him."

Jessica's heart sank. Was her father making her stay home? She looked at Marybeth and shrugged. "I've got to find out what my dad wants. Do you mind waiting a few minutes? You can put Daisy in the corral next to Rusty if you want. He always enjoys seeing her."

"Why would he ask you to unsaddle your horse?" Marybeth said in concern. "You'd better give the sandwiches to Michael to put on the ATV. Gosh, do you think your dad listened to Ariel and he's going to make us stay here?"

Jessica shook her head. "I don't know. I sure hope not."

She put the gelding back in his corral and removed his saddle and bridle. She didn't want to ride Grizz, but if it meant getting to go to the lake with all the other kids, she'd do it.

When she reached her father, she was surprised to see him standing there holding onto Storm Chaser's reins. Duncan sat on his borrowed horse with a big smile on his face.

"I thought you might like to try a new ride to the lake today." Mr. Warner offered Jessica the reins and cupped his hand to give her a boost into the saddle.

"B-but..." Jessica stammered. "I can't ride Chase. You said I wasn't ready...and she's not really broke yet. Duncan should be the one riding her." She said the words out loud, but she was dying to swing up into that saddle and smooch the filly into a ground-eating gallop.

Mr. Warner put a steadying hand on Jessica's shoulder. "Like I said, this horse is smart, just like her mama." He motioned her to step to the mounting side of the horse.

"We're not going to cut you totally loose. Duncan will be ponying you off his horse on a lead line. If there's any trouble, you two will switch horses. Understood?"

Jessica nodded.

"Well, step around here and mount up," her father said.

Jessica felt her hands begin to shake. It wasn't that she was afraid. Not really. But she'd thought about this moment ever since the paint filly had entered the holding pen with the rest of the new horses. But she'd given up all hope of ever getting to ride her.

And now, here was her big chance. She couldn't pass that up!

She accepted the reins and pulled them over Chase's head so they settled just in front of the saddle horn. Being short made it hard to reach the stirrups, so her father reached out to help boost her into the saddle.

"Go slow and easy, Jess," Duncan said as he moved in to hook a lead rope to the halter Chase wore under her bridle. "Come down on her back real easy-like and get your feet in the stirrups as quick as you can."

Jessica swung her leg over the filly's back, just like her father had taught her to do with Rusty when she first learned to ride. She settled her weight gently in the middle of the saddle and quickly found her stirrups. Then Chase shifted her weight and Jessica felt her heartbeat quicken.

"Relax, Jess." Duncan moved his horse into position on her left side, keeping Chase's head at his knee. "We're just going to pony around the barnyard a bit and make sure you're both comfortable with each other before we get out on the trails." He moved his horse forward, and Chase stepped in line beside him.

Just relax, Jessica told herself. *Breathe.*

Chase popped her head up, reminding Jessica that the reins were too tight. Jess let out several inches of rein until she barely had contact with the filly's mouth. Western horses were taught to go on a loose rein, but Chase wasn't broke enough to ride that way yet.

The other horse walked out at a pretty good pace, and Storm Chaser broke into a jig to catch up. Jessica immediately tensed and pulled back on the reins.

"Easy, Jess. I've got you. It's just a walk in the barnyard," Duncan said in a low tone, and Jessica felt herself relax. The same tone of voice he used to calm the horses also seemed to work for her. She took another deep breath and sat up straighter in the saddle. She could do this.

"That's better, Jess," Mr. Warner called from across the yard.

Marybeth came to join them. Jessica had to smile at the way her friend's mouth dropped open when she saw her riding Chase. Several of the vacationers walked up with their horses to watch, too. Jessica and her brother made another trip around the stable yard, and Mr. Warner pronounced them ready to go.

"Looks like everyone's here but Ariel and Michael," Sheri said. "The other kids are waiting for us by the trailhead."

A moment later, the sound of hoofbeats echoed across the way and Ariel galloped in on her beautiful black horse. Lainey and David had to jump back to get out of the way.

Jessica felt Chase stiffen under her as the big black horse bore down upon them. Duncan held tight to the lead line and turned Chase's head over his horse's withers. Jessica gathered a handful of mane and held on for dear life as the paint filly flipped her butt around, trying to get out of the way of the charging horse.

Ariel expertly pulled her horse down to a trot and stopped ten feet from where they stood, laughing at their reactions.

"Why did you do that?" Duncan said. He looked disgusted, but Ariel didn't seem to notice.

She tucked her long blond hair up under her helmet and smiled. "Oh, I was having a little fun, that's all. I was just trying to scare you guys."

Mr. Warner took hold of the girl's fancy English reins. "Horse safety and the safety of our guests are of utmost importance," he said. "I suggest you practice a little restraint in the future, or you won't be allowed to go on these rides."

With that, Mr. Warner turned and walked away. Jessica wanted to applaud him. Ariel's little stunt could have gotten someone hurt.

Ariel shrugged. "Your dad's awfully touchy today," she said to Duncan, but he didn't answer. "Okay, look, I'm sorry," she added quickly. "I won't do it again."

Duncan turned the horses and headed them toward the trail without saying a word.

Good, Jessica thought. She'd had enough of Ariel. And she had a feeling everyone else was getting fed up, too.

FOURTEEN

They started their morning trip at a walk so the less experienced riders could get used to traveling on horseback and the horses could get used to the ATVs. Halfway through the ride to the lake, Jessica finally relaxed enough to move with the rocking motion of Chase's steps. They even trotted for a while, and the filly behaved perfectly. Jessica felt confident enough that she began to point out various wildflowers—like bright red Indian paintbrush, big yellow balsamroot, and tiny white phlox—to their guests.

"I can't believe that all of this is out here," Sheri said. "From the road it just looks like a bunch of sagebrush and sand. Who would have thought all this really cool stuff was here?"

Marybeth turned in the saddle. "Just wait until you see the lake. You'd never know it's there, either. You come up over the rise in the mountain, and there it is, right in the middle of the desert."

Ariel trotted up beside Duncan. His gelding pinned his

ears in warning, and Raven sidestepped away. "Whoa, that's one grouchy horse," she said.

He reined in the gelding, allowing Ariel to ride up beside him and Jessica. "Sorry about that."

Ariel shrugged. "No problem." She lifted her hair off her neck. "It sure is hot here. I hope I've got enough sunscreen on." They rode in silence for a bit, until Ariel spoke again. "I wanted to go to Hawaii for vacation, but the rest of my family wanted to come here. I mean…I love horseback riding and all, and this place is okay, I guess. But it's just a bunch of gnarly old sagebrush and tons of sand with no beach. What's so great about that?"

Jessica raised an eyebrow. She didn't know much about boys, but telling them you didn't like the things they liked didn't seem like a very good way to flirt.

Duncan shrugged. "I've never been to Hawaii. Surfing would probably be pretty cool. But nothing compares to riding out across the desert in the middle of a storm."

Lainey stood in the saddle to stretch her legs. Her horse took that as a cue to go faster and broke into a trot, sitting her back in the saddle. Lainey laughed and grabbed a handful of mane, pulling her horse back to a walk. When she had the mare under control, she rode up beside Jessica. "That sure is a beautiful paint horse. Is she yours?"

Jessica shook her head. "I wish. But no, she's for sale. My family buys some horses from the reservation every year, and Duncan and our dad break them and sell them. Ranchers all over Nevada and northern California have bought our horses."

"She sure is pretty," Michael hollered from the ATV, "and smart, too." The boys were riding twenty feet away from the horses so they wouldn't spook them. But by now all the horses were used to the noise. "I can't believe your brother just broke her. That's awesome."

"Jessica did most of the work," Duncan said. "I had the easy part. All I had to do was climb on her back and go."

Jessica beamed with pride.

"How much farther to the lake?" Ariel asked.

"Not far," Marybeth said. "Just over this next hill. She squeezed Daisy's sides and cantered up the hill. "Last one there is a rotten egg!"

Jessica held on tight as Storm Chaser reacted to the Appaloosa's quick takeoff. The other kids, even Ariel, whooped and hollered up the hill. Duncan pulled the lead rope tight when Chase tossed her head and attempted to go with them.

"Hang on, Jess! Don't let her jump out from under you."

Jessica grabbed ahold of the mane and settled deep in the saddle as Chase hopped around. Once the filly figured out she couldn't go anywhere, she finally calmed down.

"Are you okay?" Duncan asked.

Jessica nodded.

"You never want to let yourself fall asleep on a young horse." He slacked off on the lead rope and let it out to a normal length. "They can jump out from under you quicker than a zephyr wind coming down the mountain."

Jessica let her breathing settle back to normal and tried to steady her nerves. "Can we try trotting up the hill?"

Duncan nodded and smooched the horses into a slow trot. Jessica gathered her reins just enough so she could feel Chase's mouth and leaned forward slightly to make it easier for Chase to get up the hill.

A few minutes later they reached the lake and found the others' horses tied to the hitching line. The kids were already pulling off riding clothes and heading into the water in their bathing suits to play with a big blow-up beach ball that Marybeth had brought.

Ariel stood at the edge of the lake. "A beach ball? What is this, the third-grade picnic?"

Marybeth halted in midthrow, looking dejectedly toward the older girl. Jessica felt sorry for her.

"Oh, come on, Ari," Michael said. "We're going to play water volleyball. Get in here and play."

"All right." Ariel kicked off her shoes and stepped into the water in her bathing suit top and shorts.

Jessica didn't miss the way Duncan's eyes swung to the beautiful girl. Ariel didn't miss it either. She laughed and called out, "Who wants to be on my team? I've got dibs on Mark and Melissa."

"Lainey, Sheri, Monica, you're with me," Michael said. "We'll smoke those guys."

"We need one more person for my team," Ariel said.

She looked briefly in Jessica's direction, but her gaze quickly swept past and landed on Duncan. She tossed the beach ball at him. "How about you?"

Duncan caught the ball and handed it to Jessica. "Jess can take my place. Marybeth and I are going to go jump off the tire swing."

Marybeth squealed in delight. She always loved playing on the tire swing with Duncan because he could push her a lot higher than Jessica could.

"What's with your brother?" Ariel asked when Jessica swam up beside her.

Jessica shrugged. "That's just the way he is. Duncan is even shy around his friends. Until he gets to know you, he really clams up."

Ariel took the ball and batted it to Sheri on the other side. "Well, we're going to be here a few more days. He'll know me by then."

Jessica shrugged. "You never know about Dunce."

"Dunce?" Lainey laughed. "Great nickname. I hope he doesn't live up to it."

Jessica tilted her head to look at Duncan playing on the tire swing with Marybeth. "Actually, he's super smart, so it doesn't really fit him."

"Let's get this game going!" Michael gave the ball a big toss and it bounced off David's head. The other boy laughed and swam for the ball, returning it with a big swat.

They messed around with the beach ball for another half hour, then everyone headed to the tire swing. Duncan went to check the horses.

"Your brother is so cool," Monica said.

"Yeah, he's not bad—for a brother." Jessica watched as Ariel swung high over the lake's surface and executed a perfect dive off the tire to show off. Jessica wished she had the kind of confidence that Ariel had. Maybe then she wouldn't be so quiet around Wyatt. She noticed Duncan watching Ariel as she swam in the lake.

They swam for a while longer, then waded out of the water, ready for something to eat.

Marybeth handed out the drinks while Jessica passed out sandwiches and apples. Monica and Sheri started a food fight, but with only one sandwich apiece, it didn't last long. The squirrels and birds would make sure the mess got cleaned up after they were gone.

"This is fun!" Marybeth said. "It's like being in school with so many kids around."

"Ha!" Ariel scoffed. "There's nothing fun about school."

"Hey, guys, it's time to head back," Duncan called, checking his watch. "There are games scheduled in about two hours and it'll take us an hour to get back to the ranch. My mom's getting some hamburgers and hotdogs ready for later."

Jessica laughed. "Yeah, after we wrecked all those sandwiches, there's going to be a lot of hungry people at dinner."

Everyone took one last dip in the lake and waded from the water, laughing and joking. They dried off quickly in the hot Nevada sun and slipped into their shorts, shirts, and shoes. Then they mounted the horses and started up the ATVs for the ride back to the ranch.

Ariel rode beside Jessica and Duncan, trying to coax Duncan into conversation. Jessica felt totally left out. Even though Ariel was so snobby, part of Jessica couldn't help wanting to be friends with her. Maybe Ariel was nice when you got to know her. It seemed like she was trying really hard to impress everyone.

Duncan gave their father a nod when they rode into the

stable yard. "Jess and Chase both did great," he reported. "I think if we keep Jess on the towline for a few more trips, and I ride Chase in between, Jess'll be able to go on her own by the end of the week."

Jessica couldn't help but grin. She was going to ride Chase again—and soon all by herself!

* * * * *

A soft tapping on the back door woke Jessica from her nap in the living room. It had been a long day filled with swimming, games, and too much to eat. After dinner she'd planned to lie down on the couch for just a few minutes, but a quick look at the clock showed she'd slept for almost an hour. Marybeth would be over in a little bit to watch their favorite TV show. They'd played horseshoes after their swim today, but there were no scheduled activities for the evening. The vacationers were free to do as they pleased.

The knock came again and Jessica swung her legs over the side of the couch. It had to be one of the guests. She walked to the door and was surprised to see Ariel standing there with a smile on her face.

"Uh...hi," Jessica stammered. "Do you need something?"

"No," Ariel said. "I'm just kind of bored and thought I'd come see what you were doing."

Jessica was dumbfounded. So far, Ariel hadn't shown much interest in being friends. Maybe she'd changed her mind?

"So can I come in?" Ariel asked.

Before Jessica even had a chance to nod, the girl squeezed her way through the door. "Do you have anything cold to drink, like a Diet Coke or something?"

"Sure." Jessica led the way to the kitchen and poured Ariel a soda. The tall blonde girl chitchatted as she roamed around the room, picking up saltshakers and sugar bowls and opening cupboards to see what was inside. Jessica knew her mother would have a fit if she ever did that while visiting someone else's house.

"Where's your brother?" Ariel asked. "I haven't seen him since we went to the lake this morning."

Now Jessica knew why Ariel was hanging around there. "He's out working on the tractor. We'll be cutting hay soon, so he's making sure everything works right and is ready to go. We lost our whole hay supply in the barn fire. We've got to get this load in the barn or we'll be in for major trouble this winter."

Ariel pulled out a chair and sat down. "At least it's a good thing that barn is getting a roof put on. I saw your dad and someone else up there working on it today."

Jessica nodded, wondering why Ariel didn't leave now that she knew Duncan wasn't here. But this might be a chance to get to know her better. They could definitely talk about horses. Jessica admired the girl's horsemanship—although she didn't always agree with the way she treated Raven.

Before Jessica could say anything, Ariel finished her drink and set the glass on the table. "Want to go for a ride with me and Raven in about a half-hour?"

"Sure!" Jessica blurted out. She wished she could ride

Chase, but she knew her dad would make her take one of the horses they'd borrowed from the Lightfoots.

"Great," Ariel said, making her way to the door. "Hey, I might even let you ride Raven for a while. We could change horses on the trail."

Jessica's head spun. She'd never been on a fancy Warmblood before. Raven was a breed of horse that you saw competing in the Olympics. Rusty was a fun ride, but he was a grade horse, with no pedigree or registration papers. The other horses at Wild Hawk Ranch were quarter horses—a great breed, but definitely not in the same category as Raven.

"Sounds great," Jessica said. Then she remembered Marybeth.

"What's the matter?" Ariel stopped with her hand on the doorknob.

"I forgot that Marybeth is coming over pretty soon. Is it okay if she goes with us?"

Ariel wrinkled her nose. "I really don't want a little kid tagging along. Can't you call her and tell her to stay home?"

Jessica hesitated. She didn't want to un-invite her friend. But she really wanted a chance to ride Raven. Nobody around had a horse like that. She might not ever get a chance like this again. Marybeth would understand. "Okay," she said.

"Good. Then I'll see you in half an hour." Ariel grabbed a cookie from a plate on the counter and left.

Jessica picked up the phone and dialed Marybeth's house. She didn't feel good about doing this, but...she did want to go with Ariel.

By the time Marybeth's phone rang a second time, Jessica felt totally guilty for dumping her friend. She almost hung up, but Marybeth's cheerful voice answered.

"Hello?"

"Um...hi," Jessica stammered as she racked her brain for something to say that wouldn't be a lie. She didn't want to fib to Marybeth.

"I just came in from saddling Daisy," her friend said. "I'll be over in a few minutes."

Jessica shifted her weight and moved the phone to the other ear. "That's what I wanted to talk to you about... uh...I've got something else that I have to do, so I won't be able to watch TV." *At least that part is true,* Jessica thought. She was definitely doing something else. "I'll just see you here tomorrow, okay? I think we're playing horseshoes again after lunch."

"Oh." Marybeth sounded disappointed. "Well, I guess I'll just ride around here by myself for a while, then. No sense wasting a saddled horse."

"Okay," Jessica said. "I'm really sorry." After she hung up, her stomach felt a little upset. She turned to see her mother standing by the couch. Jessica knew her mother had probably heard most of her conversation with Marybeth.

"Marybeth is staying home tonight?" Mrs. Warner asked.

Jessica nodded.

Her mother gave her a thoughtful look. "Well, honey, just remember: It pays to know who your real friends are." She turned and walked out of the room.

Jessica stared at the empty doorway. She knew who her

friends were, and Marybeth was one of them. But what was wrong with making new friends? It was just a stupid ride with Ariel. What could be wrong with that? Her mother had told her to be nice to the vacationers. That was exactly what she was doing.

But as she walked through the stable yard to catch the borrowed gelding, she knew she was lying to herself as well as her friend. She wasn't just being nice to Ariel. She really wanted to be friends with her. Who wouldn't? She was pretty and daring and older—and an accomplished rider.

Making friends with Ariel wouldn't be easy with Marybeth around.

FIFTEEN

The ride would have been a lot more fun if Marybeth had come along, Jessica thought as she and Ariel rode the trail back to the ranch. Once Ariel realized that Jessica wasn't allowed to ride Chase, she'd spent most of the time talking about all her friends and accomplishments at school, bragging about the ribbons she'd won at important horse shows, and asking questions about Duncan. Jessica didn't even get a chance to ride Raven. A jackrabbit had popped out in front of them and spooked the big black horse, so Ariel pronounced him unfit for a less-experienced rider to handle.

Jessica thought about mentioning the fact that her father and brother trusted her enough to ride a green-broke horse. Surely she could ride the big, well-broke Warmblood at a walk going down the trail? Yes, he was wearing an English saddle and tack, but Jessica was sure she could handle it. Ariel had a lot more experience than she did, especially with schooling lessons, but Jessica knew enough not to fall off a horse at a walk.

She gave Grizz a bump in the belly to speed up his lazy walk. The horse pinned his ears and swished his tail to show his displeasure. The ride also would have been a lot more fun if she could've ridden Rusty or Chase. At least they wouldn't have been so foul-tempered.

By the time the two girls rode into the stable yard, it was getting dark. The other visitors were getting ready for the evening snack. Jessica knew that there would be hot fudge sundaes and several kinds of pies. The mouthwatering scent of apple pie drifted out through the open kitchen window, making her stomach growl.

Her father and Duncan were climbing down from the barn roof, where they'd just put on the last piece of plywood sheeting. The girls pulled the horses to a halt at the hitching post.

"Here." Ariel dismounted and handed Raven's reins to Jessica. "Can you put Raven away for me? I've got to go do something." She started off in Duncan's direction, then called over her shoulder, "I'll save you a spot at the dessert table."

Jessica sighed, and Raven looked at her with big solemn eyes. She wanted to be mad at him for causing her extra work, but it wasn't his fault. She quickly untacked him and led the big horse to his corral, then returned for the other horse.

Jessica removed the saddle from his back, groomed him, and gave him the treats from her pocket. Then she went to the other side of the pens to see Rusty and Chase.

Rusty nickered when he saw her approach and Jessica

smiled. The old gelding definitely looked better these past few days. His burned spots had already grown new hair and he didn't cough as much anymore. "Sorry, ol' boy," she told the horse. "I've given all the treats away." Rusty nuzzled her pockets and Jessica wished she'd thought to hold back a couple of goodies.

She went to the line of trees outside the pens and pulled up several handfuls of grass. Chase stepped up to the fence and bobbed her head when she smelled the fresh green blades.

Jessica couldn't hold back a smile. Chase was coming around nicely and seemed to like people. Whoever ended up with the beautiful filly would be very lucky.

The thought made her sad. She'd grown attached to Chase, and so had Rusty. Jessica divided the grass and gave a handful to each of them, then kissed Rusty on the tip of the nose. "We're going to miss her, aren't we ol' boy?" She put her arms around his neck and breathed in his warm horse scent. Everything would work out right. She had to keep telling herself that. Chase would go to someone very special who would love her and take great care of her. Maybe even someone close by so she could go and visit.

If only Chase didn't have to go anywhere at all.

* * * * *

"Jessica?" Mrs. Warner poked her head into her daughter's room just before bedtime. "Ariel is here to see you." She opened the door wider, allowing Ariel into the room.

The girl gave Jessica a big smile and waved. "I just wanted to drop by and say thanks for taking care of Raven for me, and I'm sorry I wasn't able to save you a seat at the dessert table. Duncan got there first." She walked across the room and plopped down on the end of Jess's bed.

Jessica put down her horse magazine. It had kind of bothered her that Ariel hadn't saved her a seat. But she didn't want to say that to Ariel, and it was nice that she had come by to apologize. "No problem," she said. "Raven's a great horse. He didn't give me any trouble." She sat there for a few awkward moments, trying to think of something cool to say. Ariel saved her by speaking first.

"I was talking to the other kids and we decided to have a marshmallow roast at ten o'clock. Lainey's mom said she'd chaperone us and it's okay with your parents. I love S'mores." She bounced a little on the bed. "Do you think Duncan will come?"

Jessica tried to hide her frown. It sure seemed like Ariel asked a lot of questions about Duncan. "I don't know," she said. "He's supposed to start baling hay tomorrow and he'll have to be up really early. But I'll definitely be there." She'd have to call Marybeth and let her know. Maybe inviting her to the marshmallow roast would almost make up for dumping her earlier.

Ariel picked up one of Jessica's horse magazines and thumbed through it. "Yeah," she said in a less than enthusiastic tone. "It's just that Duncan makes things more interesting."

He does? Jessica thought, trying to hide her hurt. Sure, Ariel was almost three years older, but Jessica was trying really hard to fit in and make the older girl like her. She felt a moment of shame when she thought about Marybeth. Was this the way Marybeth felt when she was trying to fit in with *her?*

"I'm thirsty," Ariel said. "Do you think you could get me a glass of water? I really want to read this article."

"Sure," Jessica said. "I'll be right back."

She went downstairs to the kitchen and came back with a glass of ice water. But when she opened the door to her bedroom, it was empty.

"Ariel?" She paused for a moment, looking around the room. The sound of the girl's laughter came from down the hall. She followed it to Duncan's room, stopping several feet outside the door.

"You probably shouldn't even be in here," she heard her brother say.

"Why not?" Ariel said. "We're just talking. I was getting bored waiting for your sister."

Bored? Jessica's grip tightened on the glass. She'd only been gone for two minutes. How could she get bored in that amount of time? Especially since she'd left Ariel with her best horse magazines! It was becoming painfully obvious that Ariel didn't want to be friends with her at all. She was only interested in Duncan.

"Oh, hey," Duncan said, spotting Jessica in the hall. "There's Jess now." He jumped to the door, giving her a please-help-me look and pulling her into the room. Jessica almost dropped the water.

"Here," she said, handing the glass to Ariel.

"Why don't you take Ariel down and show her the map of where we're going on the cattle drive?" Duncan said.

Ariel looked disappointed as Duncan closed the door solidly behind her and Jessica. "Your brother sure is hard to get to know," she said. "Usually guys are dying to talk to me."

I bet, Jessica thought. Aloud she said, "Yeah, well, like I said, he's pretty shy."

"Good thing I like a challenge," Ariel said. "Anyway, thanks for the drink. I'll see you at the roast. We can look at the cattle drive map later." She started to leave, then turned back to Jessica. "Oh, and I know your little buddy will probably be here tonight, but try to keep the munchkin away from me, okay? She really bugs me." Ariel lifted her glass in salute and started down the hall. "And see if you can talk Duncan into showing up," she called over her shoulder.

Jessica stared after the blonde girl. She didn't understand Ariel at all. And what was she going to do about Marybeth? She knew her parents wouldn't be happy if some kind of trouble started between the kids. Maybe it would be better to leave Marybeth out of the marshmallow roast.

* * * * *

Jessica woke at 4 a.m. when she heard Duncan tiptoeing down the hall. He'd be on the tractor baling hay hours before anyone even rose for breakfast. Ariel had been a real jerk at the campfire last night when he hadn't shown up. After seeming so excited about having a marshmallow roast, Ariel had suddenly declared that s'mores were fattening and singing songs around a campfire was stupid. Apparently, if Ariel wasn't having fun, she made sure no one else would either.

Jess sat up in bed and leaned toward the window, parting the curtains. It was still dark, but the half-moon allowed her to see the clouds gathering on the horizon. She hoped it wouldn't rain. Rain was the last thing they needed when cutting hay. But if the weather stayed dry for the remainder of the summer, they wouldn't get another cutting, which they desperately needed. Either way, they would be in big trouble.

She lay back in her bed and tried to go back to sleep, but she wasn't tired. She tossed and turned a few times, then decided to get up.

"What are you doing awake so early?" her father asked when she entered the kitchen.

Jessica yawned. "I couldn't sleep. I thought maybe I could help with the hay."

Duncan handed her a piece of toast while her father poured her a glass of juice. "Well, there are some boards we'll need to move before we can get the hay in the barn," her father said. "You can help with that. Duncan's going to be running the baler, and the Lightfoot boys will follow behind him with the wagon, picking up bales. You're strong enough this year to help drag the bales off the wagon when we load them into the barn."

Jessica nodded and took a bite of her toast, eyeing Duncan's bacon hungrily. He ignored her for a few moments, then rolled his eyes and handed her two pieces off his plate.

"Thanks, Dunce," she said. "You're the best."

Mr. Warner smiled teasingly. "I know another gal who thinks the same thing."

Duncan lowered his head, and Jessica could see the red creeping into his face.

"She's Jessie's friend, not mine," Duncan mumbled.

"Not really," Jessica said. "Sometimes I think she wants to be friends, but then she starts being kind of mean."

"Especially to Marybeth," Duncan said. "Poor kid."

That made Jessica feel even worse. She still felt guilty for avoiding her friend because Marybeth bugged Ariel so much.

They quickly finished their breakfast, put the dishes in the sink, and pulled on their boots. When Mr. Warner went to find the keys to the tractor, Duncan said, "Look, Jess, I know you want some new friends and all, but watch out for Ariel, okay? I'm not really sure she wants to be friends with anybody."

"Except you," Jessica said.

"Well, you can't blame her for *that.*" Duncan playfully slugged her in the arm, then put on his hat and walked out the door.

Jessica worked by lantern for over an hour to move the boards with her father. The Lightfoots came in with the first load of hay just as the sun peeked over the hills. Wyatt looked rather sleepy, but he smiled at Jessica and helped her up onto the hay wagon before jumping down to move the hay.

"Just roll the bales off to us," Wyatt said as he pulled on his gloves and picked up his hay hooks. "We'll put it in the stack."

A low rumble of thunder sounded and Jessica cocked her

head. It was unusual to have thunder this early in the morning. That wasn't a good sign. She gazed at the mountain to the west of their ranch. Dark clouds hung low on the hillsides.

"Looks like it's going to be a race between us and Mother Nature," Gator said. "I felt a few drops on the way in with this load. I'm guessing we've got about two hours to get this hay put up before we get some serious rain. If we take too long...Mother Nature wins."

Jessica nodded, glad that she'd offered to help. It was taking all of them working together to save Wild Hawk Ranch, and they couldn't afford to lose another crop of hay.

SIXTEEN

The rains arrived just as Gator had predicted. The guests finished breakfast and, after checking their horses, retired to the bunkhouses to wait out the storm. Nevada storms were often fast and ferocious, quickly replaced with blue skies and sunshine. The guests would spend their morning inside, waiting for the sun.

Ariel made an appearance at the barn just as the rain began to fall. Jessica hoped she was there to help, as she was the only one in the barn right now. The bales weighed almost as much as she did.

"You have to move hay?" Ariel asked. "That's a tough job. We hire people to do that for us."

Jessica wiped the sweat from her forehead and nodded. "Yeah, well, it's worth it. If we lose this crop of hay, we're in a lot of trouble. And the guys are helping, too. They're out in the field getting another load."

Ariel looked around the barn, then through the open door to the fields. "Who are those new guys? The ones who were helping your dad yesterday."

"Wyatt and Gator." Jessica shoved another bale into place on the stack and sat down with a sigh. Obviously Ariel wasn't going to volunteer to help. She'd probably go right back to the bunkhouse—unless she decided to stick around and flirt with the Lightfoots as well as Jessica's brother when they returned.

"They're kind of cute." Ariel waved and smiled, then headed out the door. "See you later."

Jessica sighed. It would have been nice to have someone to help, or at least someone to talk to. But she couldn't really expect a paying guest to do a tough job like putting up hay. Ariel was on vacation.

Jessica stacked the last few bales, then pulled on her rain gear. The rain was steady now. She went to find the wagon with the boys. When she arrived, her father was giving instructions for Duncan to quit baling and help with the loading. It made no sense to bale wet hay. It would mold in the stack. Once it stopped raining, the hay that was still down in the field would have to be turned several times over the next few days so it could dry out enough to be baled again. It wouldn't look pretty and green like the rest of the hay, but it would be edible.

Luckily, Duncan had already baled most of the field, but they needed to get those bales in the barn. Mr. Warner hooked his truck up to a second wagon and they all worked together to save the crop.

Jessica wiped the rain from her eyes. Small bits of hay stuck to her wet clothes and cheeks as she dragged the bales that Gator tossed up onto the wagon. Her hair lay plastered to her head, and she knew she looked a mess. But Wyatt still smiled at her every time she pulled a bale of hay over for him to stack. He probably felt sorry for her.

A horn sounded and Jessica turned to see Marybeth and her father bumping across the hay field. They pulled their truck alongside the wagon, and Marybeth's father rolled down the window. "We thought you folks might need some help," he said.

"Every spare hand is welcome." Mr. Warner said, motioning for their neighbor to park his truck and join them.

Jessica grinned broadly at Marybeth as she reached down to pull her friend onto the wagon. It wasn't just that she was glad to have the help. She was genuinely happy to see Marybeth. She still felt bad about leaving her out the night before.

"Hey, check this out!" Duncan pointed to the edge of the field. A crowd of people walked toward them in the rain.

Jessica was surprised to see their guests waving and smiling as they drew closer to the hay wagons. She noticed that Ariel wasn't among the group.

"We're here to help," Lainey said as she held up a hay hook. "We're not sure what we're doing, but we'll give it a try."

Michael grabbed a bale from Duncan and tossed it onto the wagon. "We know how important it is that you get this crop in the barn."

Mr. Warner clapped him on the back. "Thank you, son." He turned to the rest of the group. "Thank you all. This means a lot to us. Now let's load some hay!"

A few hours later, Jessica gazed at the bales of hay scattered all over the floor of the barn to air dry. Tomorrow, they'd put them in the stack.

It had been a lot of hard work, but it was worth it. They'd had fun, even though everyone eventually got soaked while they joked and picked up the hay. When they were done, everyone voted to take the rest of the day off, even Duncan and Mr. Warner. They needed to be rested for tomorrow when preparations would begin for the cattle drive.

Jessica couldn't wait.

* * * * *

The following morning, Jessica trotted Chase around the training pen, gazing at the beautiful blue sky. Yesterday's hard rain seemed like a dream, except for all the drying bales of hay in the barn. Duncan had gotten up early to turn the hay, but now he was shouting directions to her from the center of the ring. Jessica tried hard to do what he asked.

"If you're going to try to ride this filly on the cattle drive, you better know how to keep her under control," Duncan called. "She's not a finished horse, Jess. She still doesn't know all the cues and how to respond. You'll need to use a little more rein and a lot more leg on her in the beginning. She's not 'push-button' like our old horses."

Jessica saw a flash of blonde hair streak toward the training pen. Ariel. *Great. This was just what she needed…a professionally trained rider to watch her practice riding Chase.* She hoped she wouldn't embarrass herself by making stupid mistakes or getting bucked off.

Ariel stepped up and leaned on the round pen rail. "So, how is Jessica doing?"

She spoke directly to Duncan, but he only responded in short answers, giving most of his attention to Jessica and Chase.

"That sure is a nice paint," Ariel tried again. "She looks like she comes from good stock."

Bingo! That was all it took to get Duncan talking. Jessica saw his impatient look turn to interest, and he rattled off Chase's lineage.

"Wow," Ariel said. "So she's a papered horse and the Lightfoots turned her out on pasture to run wild?"

"Just while she was growing," Duncan said. "She's not a mustang. It's a pretty common practice, even with big-time trainers. We don't keep our horses boxed up in stalls all their lives."

"Hmmm," Ariel said. "So is she for sale, then? This filly is pretty enough to show. I've been bugging my parents for another horse. I've wanted to try showing western pleasure, and Raven just isn't the horse for that."

"Yeah, she's for sale," Duncan said. "You'd have to talk to my dad about price and stuff."

Jessica wanted to bean her brother with a cow chip. Sure, she knew that Chase would be sold eventually, but she didn't want the filly to go to Ariel. She'd load Storm Chaser into her trailer and take her a zillion miles away.

"All right, Jess, that's enough," Duncan called. "Walk her for a few minutes to cool her down, then put her away." He walked to the gate and let himself out. "I think you two will be fine on the cattle drive. Just be sure you stay with one of the better riders. After a few miles, Chase will settle in."

"Don't worry, I'll keep an eye on her," Ariel volunteered.

Duncan nodded and walked to the corral to get another horse.

Wonderful, Jessica thought. *Ariel has everything she could possibly need, and now she's showing an interest in the only horse I want.* She dismounted and led the filly to the hitching post, where she pulled her saddle and bridle and gave her a quick sponge bath. "We're going to do just fine on the cattle drive," she said to Chase, even though she wasn't sure she believed it. "We're going to have lots of fun, and I'm not going to be nervous at all."

She pulled an apple from her pocket and fed it to the filly, then turned her loose in the corral with Rusty. "I've got one for you too, buddy." She gave him the apple and laid her cheek on his neck. "I wouldn't be sweating bullets if it were you I was riding," she confided to the old gelding. She gave him a hug and headed up to the house to help her mom start packing the chuck wagon. They'd be off on their cattle drive by day after tomorrow. She'd call Marybeth tonight and remind her friend about all the things she'd need for the trip.

* * * * *

"Let's go. We're burnin' daylight!" Mr. Warner shouted, signaling to the riders to move the cattle out of the fields and onto the trail. David and Michael rode their ATVs and stayed well toward the back, but the rest of the vacationers were on horseback and stationed at various spots around the herd.

Jessica sat atop Chase in the early morning light, listening to the sounds of the new day. Cattle lowed and calves bawled as they set hooves to the dusty trail. Scrub jays flitted among the sagebrush, picking at bugs and chattering to each other. Shep barked and heeled cattle, helping to move them along the path.

Jessica put a steadying hand on Chase's neck as the filly danced around, eager to be off with the rest of the horses. She could feel the paint's muscles quiver under her palm. "It's okay, girl. There's nothing to be afraid of." She felt the rush of adrenaline though her veins and wondered if she was the one who needed the pep talk, not Chase.

"There you are." Marybeth rode up on Daisy. "Most of the cattle are on the trail. Don't you want to catch up to everyone? " She looked at Jessica more closely. "Are you okay? You don't look so good."

Jessica bit her lip. "I'm okay, but I'm a little..."

"Scared?" Marybeth finished.

"Yeah," Jessica admitted, pulling Chase in a small circle and trying to get her under better control. "A little, anyway," she added in a shaky voice. "What if Chase really acts up and I can't control her? She's getting a little crazy right now."

"She'll be okay," Marybeth assured her, moving Daisy into position beside Chase. "Just walk beside us until you get brave again. Some of the other riders are kind of scared, too, I think. But they're doing fine. All the horses are a little frisky this morning."

Jessica nodded and walked Chase alongside Daisy. The paint chomped at the bit and wanted to trot, but she paid attention to Jessica's signal for a walk. They joined Lainey, Monica, and Sheri at the back of the herd. The adults rode alongside with Duncan and the Lightfoot boys, asking questions and getting pointers about the cattle.

Most of the people were experienced riders, but they'd never worked with cattle. Jessica knew that the talks her father and Duncan had given them over the last few days had probably helped, but no one could be expected to remember that much information once they were on the move.

Jessica felt like she should know more about cattle drives herself. After all, she lived here on the ranch. But this morning she felt just as green as the dudes from the city.

After a bit, Mr. Warner cantered toward Jessica and the others. He pulled his horse to a walk and motioned for everyone to pay attention. "I want you people to stay here at the back for a while. In another hour or so, we'll move everyone around to a different station so you get to ride on all sides of the herd. Okay? Mrs. Warner went on ahead with the chuck wagon and will be meeting us at the first stop for lunch."

They all nodded.

"Wyatt is going to be riding back here with you also," Mr. Warner said. "If you have any questions or problems, he's your go-to man. And if he asks you to do something, I expect you to do it. The object of this drive is to keep the cattle together and keep them from spooking."

At the mention of Wyatt's name, Marybeth looked over at Jessica and wiggled her eyebrows. Jessica rolled her eyes and tried to pretend she wasn't interested.

"Jess?" Her father said. "Ariel made a special request for you to join her. She's at the front point of the herd with Duncan.

I'll ride up there with you since you're on a green horse. If Chase starts acting up, I want you to switch horses with your brother. Understand?"

Jessica nodded. But why did Ariel want her riding with her? She had Duncan all to herself. So why did she need her there, too? In spite of her doubts, Jessica's hopes rose. Maybe Ariel did want to be friends after all.

"I can go, too," Marybeth volunteered.

"That's okay," Jessica said. "Why don't you stay here to help the rest of the girls? I'll see what Ariel wants and come right back." She reined Chase into position behind her father and followed him to the head of the herd.

"There you are!" Ariel said as she waved Jessica to the spot beside her.

A small calf suddenly broke from the herd and gamboled toward them, bucking and playing. Mr. Warner grabbed hold of Chase's reins to stay her. Raven snorted loudly and bolted, giving a small hop along the way. Ariel let out a shriek, but gathered her reins and sat deep in the saddle, bringing the big horse under control.

Jessica was impressed. Except for the scream, Ariel had actually handled the incident well. Jess wondered if she could stay astride if Chase bolted like that.

Ariel brought her mount back alongside Chase and kept him on a tight rein until he settled down. "Good job," Duncan told her, flashing her an admiring look before he turned his attention back to the herd.

"Gee, he actually said something to me." Ariel smiled. "About time."

"There are other people here besides Duncan, you know,"

Jessica said, her voice sounding whiny even to her own ears.

"Yes, but none of them are as cute," Ariel said.

"Whatever," Jessica said.

Duncan tipped his hat to the girls. "I've got to ride over to the back of the herd and make sure Wyatt's not having trouble with that bossy cow that's always acting up. Chase seems to be doing fine, Jess. If you have problems, Dad's not far away."

"And there's me," Ariel added.

"Right." Duncan put his heels to his mount and cantered off.

Chase jumped around a bit, wanting to go with the other horse, but Jessica balanced herself in the saddle and tightened her reins, bringing the filly back under control. She wanted to show Ariel that she was a decent rider, too.

They rode in silence for several minutes. Laughter floated on the wind from the back of the herd. It sounded like Lainey. "Guess they're having fun," Jessica said to Ariel. "Do you want to go back there and ride with them?"

Ariel shook her head. "Nope."

Jessica touched her boot to Chase's side, asking her to move over and give Raven more room. The paint filly flicked her tail, letting Jessica know the cue was too strong, but she did as asked.

"That is such a cute little filly," Ariel said. "I think I could use her in a Hunter Class. She moves really nicely. And I told Duncan I've been wanting to try Western Pleasure. I talked to my dad about it last night. He said he'd definitely think about buying her."

Jessica almost fell out of the saddle as she felt her world tilt. Ariel was serious! But she *couldn't* buy Chase. She already had a perfect horse. Why did she need two?

Her throat tightened. This couldn't be happening. It wasn't fair! What could she do to keep Chase from falling into Ariel's hands?

SEVENTEEN

"You don't want this filly," Jessica told Ariel, her brain spinning like a tractor tire in a mud bog, trying to come up with a good excuse. "She's not a broke horse yet, and besides…you've got Raven. He's awesome."

Ariel's eyes narrowed. "Oh, I get it. You just want to keep Chase for yourself!"

"Who wouldn't?" Jessica retorted. She didn't care if she was being rude to a guest. She was fed up with Ariel. And there was no way she'd let her own Storm Chaser.

Ariel swung Raven around, reining him in a half-circle. "Your dad and Duncan said the filly is for sale. If I want to buy her, I'll buy her. And, from the looks of your ranch, you obviously need the money."

Jessica flushed in anger, but she held her tongue. She wanted to tell the older girl off, but she knew how disappointed her parents would be if she was rude to a guest, especially when that guest was a potential buyer for one of their horses. And besides, she didn't like the idea of acting just as mean and low as Ariel.

She turned in the saddle and looked back. Marybeth and some of the other kids were laughing and having a good time. That's where she should be. Not up here wasting time with an ungrateful brat like Ariel.

"I'm going to talk to Duncan again," Ariel said. "I'm sure *he'll* be interested in finding a buyer for Chase."

Duncan was riding about twenty-five yards ahead of them now. Jessica watched as the girl trotted up beside him. Her brother's horse pinned his ears and snaked his head around, trying to nip Raven when they approached. Raven jumped to the side and snorted.

Jessica wondered if it was such a good idea for Ariel to ride the high-spirited horse on this trip. Warmbloods weren't exactly cut out to do cattle drives. Everyone but Ariel and Jessica rode a well-broke, even-tempered quarter horse. But Chase was green broke, and Raven was jumpy. They were the two most unpredictable horses in the group. At the moment, Jessica noted with satisfaction, Chase was behaving better than Raven.

She leaned forward and patted the filly on the neck. She wanted to go back and join the others—especially now that Wyatt was riding with them. But her father had asked her to come up here with Ariel, and they needed someone in each position so the cattle wouldn't be tempted to stray from the herd.

Just then a cow and calf broke loose and began to wander away from the herd. "Jess, go real easy and get to the other side of that cow before she gets too far out," Duncan called back as he turned his horse to help. "Push them toward the herd, but be gentle about it."

Jessica nodded nervously. She prayed that Chase wouldn't get excited and run off with her, or spook if the cow and calf ran.

"I'll help," Ariel said, turning away from Duncan. She gave Raven a boot in the sides and pointed him toward the cow and calf.

Jessica almost had the pair back into the herd, but when the cow saw the big black horse bearing down on them, she took her calf and bolted.

To Jessica, what happened next felt like a slow motion scene from a movie. Raven gave a big jump over a clump of sagebrush, then crow-hopped several times before stumbling into a rabbit hole and falling to his knees. Ariel tumbled over his shoulder into the soft sand, then immediately got up and grabbed his reins so he wouldn't run off.

Excited, Chase jumped around, tossing her head. Jessica knew better than to take a chance on a green-broke horse. She immediately dismounted before she was tossed. "Easy," she said to Chase, attempting to calm the young filly.

Mr. Warner cantered over to Ariel. "Are you okay, young lady?"

She nodded and spoke in a shaky voice. "I…I'm fine, but I don't think Raven is. You've got to help him." She looked around. "Where are my parents?"

The black horse danced around at the ends of his reins, limping on his front right leg.

"Can he put any weight on it?" Mr. Warner asked.

Duncan rode up and dismounted, handing his reins to Jessica. He put a steadying hand on the black horse and knelt to feel his leg. "He took a pretty good tumble," Duncan said, running a practiced hand up and down Raven's leg, "but I don't feel anything broken. It doesn't look like he pulled a tendon. I'd say it's just a sprain." He looked at Ariel. "Are you okay? That was a pretty bad fall for you, too."

She brushed the sand off her pants. "I'm fine, but what about Raven? Will I be able to show him? There's a big show coming up next month."

Jessica couldn't believe her ears. Ariel should be happy that Raven hadn't broken his leg. Forget the horse show. The girl was lucky to still have a horse.

Mr. and Mrs. Wilson cantered over from the other side of the herd. Ariel's mother bailed off her horse and ran to her daughter's side. "We saw what happened, honey. Are you all right?"

Ariel nodded. "Stupid rabbit hole! We would've gotten those cows before Jessica if Raven hadn't fallen into it."

"Now, honey," her mother cajoled as she wiped the dirt from Ariel's face. "Let's not worry about that right now. Let's get your horse taken care of."

Jessica was dumbfounded. This wasn't a competition. And how could Ariel be more concerned about beating her to the cows than she was about her own horse?

"Well, it looks like this poor fella is done for a while," Ariel's father said as he ran a comforting hand over Raven's neck. "How are we going to get him back to the ranch? There's no road, so we can't get a horse trailer up here."

"He'll have to be walked back by hand," Mr. Warner said. "Give him some time to rest. We always carry an emergency kit with us. We've got a support bandage we can put on that leg to help him out a bit."

"But it's at least five miles back to the barn," Ariel complained. "That's going to take forever."

"I'll go with you," her mother said. "You should go back and rest, too. Maybe we should call the doctor out?"

Ariel put her hands on her hips. "But I don't want to go back," she said. "This is the best part of the trip. I don't want to miss it! I'm fine."

"Your mom's right. Maybe you should go back and have the doctor look at you," Duncan said. "You took a pretty good spill."

"No!" Ariel stomped her foot. "I'm finishing this cattle drive! We paid good money for this trip and this is the best part of it."

Incredible, Jessica thought. Ariel obviously didn't give a hoot about her horse. All she worried about was not missing the cattle drive and being near Duncan. And now that Raven was injured, she didn't even have a horse to ride.

Ariel turned to Mr. Warner. "You know, I've been talking to my father about buying Storm Chaser. Maybe Jessica could walk Raven back to the ranch and I could try the paint out for the rest of the cattle drive?"

Jessica clenched the reins tightly. *What a weasel!* Chase shook her head, telling her that the grip was too tight. "Sorry, girl." She let up on the reins and patted the filly's neck. Her father glanced her way and Jessica could see that this battle was lost before it even began.

The riders at the back of the herd finally caught up to them, and everyone gathered around to see what happened.

"Oh, my gosh!" Marybeth said when they heard the story. "That's terrible!"

"And now Jessica has to give up her horse to Ariel?" Monica whispered in a voice loud enough for Jessica to hear.

Jessica could feel all eyes on her and Ariel.

Mr. Warner turned to his daughter. "What do you say, Jess? I know how much you've looked forward to this ride, but we've got to get this horse back to the barn. And Ariel wants to try out the filly."

"I'll take him back," Wyatt volunteered from atop his horse. He looked at Jessica and gave her a sympathetic smile.

Tears pricked the backs of Jessica's eyes. She was grateful to Wyatt for making the offer, but he was too valuable to leave the drive. If the cattle turned surly, they'd need every experienced hand they could get. She couldn't let him do it—even if it meant Ariel riding Chase and falling in love with her.

She took a deep breath, hoping her voice wouldn't come out shaky when she spoke. "Thanks, Wyatt, but I'll take Raven back to the barn. You're too good a cowhand to lose. They need you on this trip. I'm not much help." She dismounted and handed Chase's reins to her father. There was no way she'd give them to Ariel.

"Wait, Jess," Marybeth said. "I'll go with you."

"That's really nice, Marybeth, but you wanted to go on this cattle drive more than any of us. And you worked really hard helping us get everything ready at the ranch. You deserve to go," Jessica said.

Marybeth shrugged. "I don't mind. I can go on the next cattle drive."

Jessica didn't know what to say. Even though she'd treated Marybeth badly, trying to be friends with Ariel, Marybeth was still willing to give up something she really wanted in order to help Jessica out. Now she really *did* feel like crying. She'd been such a jerk.

Mr. Warner patted Jessica on the back. "Thank you, Jess. I know you'd rather stay here and have fun." He glanced at Marybeth. "But you'll have good company. I'll call your mom on the cell phone and let her know you're on your way back with an injured horse. She'll drive the horse trailer as far as she can up the mountain to pick you up."

"I'll go back with them," Mrs. Warner said.

"No, Mom, it's fine," Jessica said. "I've ridden this trail a gazillion times. We'll be fine. Besides, Marybeth's mom will meet us a few miles down the trail."

Mrs. Warner handed Jessica her cell phone. "Take this and call if you have any trouble. Someone will be there as quickly as possible."

"Thanks, Mom." Jessica took the phone. She waited while Duncan wrapped Raven's injured leg, then she and Marybeth headed back down the mountain on foot at a very slow pace.

When they were a few minutes down the path, Jessica took a deep breath and turned to Marybeth. "Marybeth, I owe you a really big apology. I've been an idiot the last few days and I haven't paid much attention to you because I was trying to be friends with Ariel. I'm really sorry."

Marybeth shrugged. "That's okay," she said. "At first I wanted to be friends with her, too, but now I'm glad she didn't like me."

They both laughed.

"Forget about Ariel," Marybeth said. "The other kids are nice. And there'll be even more kids to meet when the next bunch of vacationers come in. Besides, there'll always be girls like Ariel. She doesn't care who she has to hurt in order to get what she wants."

Jessica turned and patted Raven. "Yeah, imagine not really caring about a horse like this." She took a deep breath. "And now she wants Chase."

"What?" Marybeth's head snapped around. Daisy jumped at the sudden movement. "Easy, girl," Marybeth cooed, calming her horse down.

"That's part of why I'm taking Raven back to the ranch," Jessica said. "It'll give Ariel a chance to try Chase out. She's already talked to her dad about buying her." They walked several more steps in silence. "You know she's going to love her," she added miserably. "How could anyone not like that filly? She's totally awesome!"

Marybeth led Daisy down a deer path on the side of the mountain, trying to find the easiest way to get Raven to the bottom. The horse was limping pretty badly, but he was managing with a few grunts and groans. Hopefully, her mother would meet them with the trailer soon. "Just don't think about it right now," she said to Jessica.

"Okay," Jessica agreed.

But she knew that would be impossible.

*****

Marybeth's mom met the girls a couple miles down the trail and they were able to get Raven safely back to the ranch and call the vet. Dr. Altom declared that the horse had a sprain and would need a few months of rest to recover.

Jessica was glad Raven was going to be fine, but she wished she hadn't had to let Ariel ride Chase.

The next twenty-four hours while they waited for everybody to return from the cattle drive seemed like forever to Jessica. Lainey and Monica called her every couple of hours on their cell phones to let her know what was happening. Ariel seemed to be doing fine on Chase, and Duncan was giving her pointers.

Jessica pursed her lips. Her brother was a traitor. He knew how much Chase meant to her. He didn't have to make it easier for Ariel to buy the paint, no matter how much their family needed the money.

She visited Rusty's pen often, brushing him and telling him about Ariel and how she was afraid the girl would take Chase away from them. She was now convinced that the only reason Ariel had taken such an interest in the filly was to get Duncan's attention.

She scratched Rusty up under his mane. "You'll miss Chase as much as I will, won't you, old boy?" She took a carrot out of her pocket and broke it into pieces to feed to the gelding.

She heard footsteps coming down the barn path and turned to see Marybeth running toward her.

"They're coming!" Marybeth pointed toward the mountain. "I saw a big cloud of dust on the high trail from my house."

They ran to the barn loft to get a better view. "It's them, all right." Jessica shaded her eyes from the setting sun. Her stomach was churning. It wouldn't be long before she'd have to hear about Ariel buying Chase and taking her far away.

She let out an exasperated breath. It really stunk to be a kid and not get any say in the matter. She had to keep reminding herself that they needed the money that Chase's sale would bring. And Ariel's parents had the cash to buy her.

Jessica looked back at the house. Her mother had returned last night after she'd fed the whole crew. She'd sympathized with Jessica and held her while she cried, but in the end, her mother had reminded her that selling Chase was necessary to help keep Wild Hawk Ranch afloat.

"I'd better go tell my mom so she can put the steaks on the grill," Jessica said. "They're going to be awfully hungry when they get back."

She and Marybeth climbed down the ladder and ran to the house. Mrs. Warner had all kinds of dinner chores to keep them busy until the riders returned. Jessica tried not to think of Chase as she husked the corn and wrapped potatoes in tinfoil to put in the oven for the welcome-home feast.

By the time the riders entered the stable yard, dinner was almost ready to serve. Jessica and Marybeth helped the tired cowhands unsaddle their horses and put them away.

"So what did you think?" Jessica asked Lainey.

Lainey stretched her tired legs. "I think I'm going to be

permanently bowlegged, but other than that, it was awesome!"

The rest of the riders agreed—even the two boys on the ATVs.

"We got to see a lot of deer and jackrabbits, and even a bighorn sheep," Michael said. "Your dad said that's pretty rare around here."

Jessica helped Monica unsaddle her horse. She glanced at Chase as Ariel dismounted and her heart squeezed in her chest. Ariel didn't look back at her as she handed Chase to Mr. Warner to unsaddle.

Wyatt led his horse to the water trough. "Hey, chin up, Jess."

She didn't feel like putting her chin up, even for Wyatt. She felt like crying.

As she unsaddled Monica's horse, the ungrateful wretch turned and nipped her when she loosened the cinch. Jessica was so distracted that she barely felt it.

"Jess, come get your horse," her father called. He held out Chase's reins for her.

Jessica frowned. *Couldn't he see how miserable she was?*

Duncan pushed her hands away from the saddle and pointed toward Chase. He had a funny smile on his face, but she couldn't see anything worth smiling about. "You heard Dad. Get going," he said.

Her legs felt like fence posts as she walked toward her father. A tear escaped down her cheek and she quickly wiped it away before anyone could see. She *would not* cry in front of all these people!

Marybeth walked beside her for a few steps and squeezed her hand. "It'll be okay, Jess. Be brave."

"Come get your horse, young lady," her father repeated.

Jessica knit her brows in confusion. Why was everyone smiling? Everyone except Ariel, who stomped away from the crowd and headed toward the bunkhouses.

When she got to Chase, Jessica reached out a shaky hand and took the reins from her father.

She put her forehead to Chase's and inhaled her warm horse scent, promising herself again that she wouldn't cry. She looked up at her father, expecting to see a look of pity in his eyes. But instead, her father was smiling down at her. Didn't he know how much it would hurt her to load the paint filly into the Wilsons' trailer with Raven?

"Better get this little gal brushed and back in the corral with Rusty where she belongs. She's had a long couple of days," Mr. Warner said.

"But she doesn't belong here anymore," Jessica said. "She'll be going home with the Wilsons."

"Now who told you that?" her father said.

Jessica stared at the dirt beneath her boots. "Ariel's parents said they'd buy her the horse."

Her father pulled the saddle from Chase's back. "Well now, honey, I've been thinking. Money isn't everything." He shrugged. "Besides, we're booked full for the entire summer with vacationers. The way I see it, this filly will be a fine addition to the ranch, and her future foals will bring a good price. Besides, you're going to need a decent horse to get any work done around here."

Jessica swallowed hard. Was her father saying…?

Mr. Warner took off his hat. "Jess, you did a really grown-up thing when you agreed to take Ariel's horse back to the ranch. And you've been working hard at training the filly and helping out around the ranch. All that made me realize how much you've grown up lately."

Jessica was speechless.

"Chase is all yours, honey. You've earned her. Now get her on back to the corral before I change my mind," her father said. "We're all looking forward to that welcome-home dinner."

Jessica couldn't believe her good fortune. Marybeth had forgiven her, and now Chase would be hers and Rusty's forever and ever!

Duncan tipped his hat to her. "You deserve it, Jess."

Marybeth slapped Jessica a high-five, and Wyatt gave her a big hug as everyone clapped and congratulated her. This would definitely be a welcome-home dinner.

Storm Chaser was home to stay for good.

ABOUT THE AUTHOR

CHRIS PLATT has been riding horses since she was two years old. At the age of sixteen, she earned her first gallop license at a racetrack in Salem, Oregon. Several years later, she became one of the first women jockeys in that state. Chris's other horse-related occupations have included training Arabian endurance horses and driving draft horses.

After earning a journalism degree from the University of Nevada in Reno, she decided to combine her love of horses with her writing. Her previous books include *Moon Shadow, Willow King, Race the Wind,* and many titles in the popular *Thoroughbred* series.

Chris lives in Nevada with her husband, six horses (two of them paints), three cats, a parrot, and a potbellied pig.

AUTHOR'S NOTE

The paint horse has a long and proud history. This breed is known for its strong stock-type body, athletic ability, and agreeable disposition. In 1519, the Spanish explorer Hernando Cortez had two pinto-colored horses in his entourage. By the 1800s, the American plains were teeming with horses, many of them loudly colored. Because of their splashy color and athletic performance, these horses became a favorite of the American Indians.

Throughout the 1800s and 1900s, paint horses grew in number. They were called pinto, paint, skewbald, and piebald. In 1962 the American Paint Stock Horse Association (APSHA) was formed to preserve the breed's stock-type conformation and color. In May 1965, the organization merged with the American Paint Quarter Horse Association to become the American Paint Horse Association (APHA). To date, there are more than 460,000 paint horses registered throughout the world.

To be registered with the APHA, foals must be of paint, quarter horse, or Thoroughbred background and have one parent registered with the APHA. Any other bloodlines must be registered as pinto.

Each paint horse has a particular coat pattern of white and any of the regular equine colors: black, bay, brown, chestnut, dun, grullo, sorrel, palomino, buckskin, gray, and roan. Markings may be of any size and shape and are found anywhere on the horse's body.

Paint horses have three main types of coat patterns:

Tobiano (tow-bee-yah-no) Marks are regular and round, usually covering one or both flanks, the neck, and the chest. The head is colored the same as a non-paint horse with blazes and snips. The tail is often two colors and all four legs are usually white.

Overo (oh-vair-oh) The white color rarely crosses the back of the horse from withers to tail. At least one and often all four legs are dark. White markings are splashy and irregular. The head markings are distinct, often with a bald or apron face. The tail is usually one color.

Tovero (tow-vair-oh) The ears and often the forehead are dark. One or both eyes are blue. This horse frequently has dark coloring around its mouth, which may extend up the side of the face. There are dark spots on the neck, flank spots, and at the base of the tail.

For more information on paint horses, visit the APHA website at www.apha.com.